I0685820

My Dead World 5

JACQUELINE DRUGA

My Dead World 5 by Jacqueline Druga

Copyright © 2023 Jacqueline Druga

Published by Vulpine Press in the United Kingdom in 2023

ISBN: 978-1-83919-541-9

Cover by Claire Wood

www.vulpine-press.com

A NOTE FROM THE AUTHOR

When I first came up with the idea for *My Dead World*, it was supposed to be one book, journal style entries from multiple points of view about the rising dead apocalypse. Well, as you know that didn't happen and here we are in book five.

It saddens me that this is the final book in the *My Dead World* Series, but all good things must come to an end. Who knows, maybe there'll be a spin off. In any event, the first section of this book is slightly different as it incorporates the narrative from the views of Nila, Sean, and Fleck.

Just the first part. You may wonder why I chose this style—I did so, so you the reader could get a good mindset of these characters as they navigate the end of this tale.

Thank you for reading this far. I hope you have enjoyed reading these books as much as I did writing them, and I truly hope you are satisfied when you reach the final page.

PART ONE

TO HOME

ONE

TRAUMA

Nila
October 5

My heart broke.

I was second guessing myself with painful memories each time my eyes closed. Memories I felt and saw vividly.

How? How did it happen?

As a leader on my homeland, did I fail, or was there really nothing I could do?

My mind still couldn't comprehend all that happened. Not in that short span of time and not to the people I loved most.

Our camp was hit in a different way, and I was facing the emotional consequences of my actions in this new world.

It wasn't even a bad day to begin with.

My testing at The Colony revealed that not only was I having twins, but one of them was immune. The other, however, was carrying the virus. A fact Ben quickly dismissed as another ploy.

Then Katie said something in the car that didn't register in the moment, but should have.

My gifted, insightful, filterless, bearer of only bad news daughter, said, "Bella doesn't need the cure anymore. Is that positive, Mommy?"

I told her it was, and I was proud. Sean and I had been trying to convince Katie to find nicer ways to say things.

In hindsight, we should have set up guidelines because Bella turning would have been an exception. There was no nice way to talk about something like that. But in her own 'new nice' way, Katie told us Bella had turned.

Something I only realized when we got back.

Ben was assuring me about the twins, Fleck was complaining again about kid mountain. And as I started to get excited, I wanted to share the news with Bella. After all, she'd been with us a year and was a great teenager. Such a good girl.

I went to her camper and heard one-year-old Christian crying. I didn't think much of it, even after I climbed inside.

Bella was on the floor by the bed, looking under it. The mother in me thought the baby had crawled under and was stuck. When I called out to Bella, she stopped, turned around, and I knew. Not only was she infected, she'd turned, and at that instant she raged towards me. After struggling with my revolver, without thought or hesitation, I killed her. My focus was on the baby and when I got to him, he was covered in blood.

The cure, The Colony, we had to head back.

Fleck radioed them and, with Ben and I in the back with Christian, Sean drove like a madman to get us there.

No matter how hard Ben tried to save the baby, he too turned and came back with a vengeance, attacking Ben.

That was my most traumatic moment for me, and I had a lot of them.

How did I do it? In the moment I didn't think, but afterward that's all I did.

Think.

With the virus now at the cabin, Sean went with Almada to get the others to bring them back and be ready to get the cure.

Doctor Rosen had me on bed rest, and gave me a sedative.

Eventually it would cause me to sleep but as it moved through my veins, making my body increasingly heavy and tired, I slipped back to thinking of that moment in the car with Christian.

I was told it had to be done. But in my heart and soul, I couldn't justify it.

How was it even possible that two competent and able-bodied adults couldn't pull a toddler from Ben's ear? Sean and I tried. Hell, even Ben was trying, but Christian was relentless in his infected state, and I took action.

I ended it.

Laying in that hospital bed I could still feel that knife in my hand and the vibration and resistance as I plunged it into Christian.

I couldn't close my eyes, because every time I did, that moment replayed over and over. It was vivid and I felt it send tremors through me. So much so it gave muscle memory a new meaning.

Struggling with what I had done, racked with guilt. I hoped whatever they gave me would kick in and help me sleep. I needed to hear Lev's voice in my head, hear him tell me it was all right. But no voice was there. I felt empty and lost and knew even if I did sleep, I'd wake up feeling the same way.

I had done some terrible things in the name of survival and for my family, but this felt different.

Eventually that feeling would go away, leaving me with just the memory to cringe at.

Until then I inwardly and silently wept for Bella, for Christian, and the godforsaken world my babies were about to enter.

TWO

PAIN

Sean

When I was seventeen, a senior in high school, I had my own car. My grandfather had given it to me when I was sixteen. It didn't run, the battery was dead, and the tires were smooth. It was my responsibility to get it up and running. I worked at a restaurant as a busboy and saved up my money. Each weekend buying a new part, and learning how to fit it from my grandfather.

By the time we were done with it, the car was pretty impressive, and I ended up learning a lot in the process of fixing it up. So much so that when I saw the principal, Mrs. Stowell, standing by her car in the school lot with the hood open, I of course offered help.

"Oh, thank you, Sean," she said to me. "I know you are good with cars."

And I was. But I was used to older models, and Mrs. Stowell had a much newer one. Still, I gave it my best shot.

I ran through the obvious things, alternator, starter, battery.

Nothing. The car wouldn't turn over.

Then it hit me.

She was out of gas.

She thought I was brilliant for making that diagnosis, and if I were right, she'd buy me a snack from the à la carte cafeteria line every day for a week.

Hey, I wasn't a fool, I'd take those snacks.

Mrs. Stowell didn't know me because I had some sort of a bad reputation, quite the opposite really, she knew me as the kid who had planned his life to a tee.

Two or three years in the Army, then off to be a police officer. I knew what I wanted to do.

So, it made sense that she felt comfortable asking this particular student of hers for a ride to the gas station and back. She felt she could count on me. And while I really didn't want to have my principal in my car, I knew she needed my help. So, I took her.

My car was clean, which we were both thankful for, but it was just weird having her in the front seat. She looked oddly out of place there. Conversation was stale and stupid, and largely centered around what I liked to watch on television. It was awkward and uncomfortable, and even though I knew I was doing a good thing—the right thing—it was still…weird.

Riding in the car with Almada felt much the same way.

Almada was a scientist from The Colony, who volunteered to accompany me back to the cabin to get the others, so they could get treatment if they were indeed infected with the virus.

Chances are they were.

Except Katie, of course; she was immune.

With Bella having it, someone else surely did.

The Colony had the cure and Almada came with me to convince the others, or rather convince Fleck, that they had to go.

Fleck.

The most hardheaded, son of a bitch I had ever met, and I'd met a lot of people in my life.

He hated me and didn't trust me. The man questioned my every move. I got it, I understood, but at some point, enough was enough.

Now like some sort of coward, I relied on Almada to talk to him. However, the price to pay was her riding in the car with me.

It was a great SUV, better than my beater Betsy, but comfortable or not, it was awkward. I actually would have preferred to talk about the virus and the undead, but like Mrs. Stowell she wanted to talk about books and television shows she missed.

She didn't ask me about the people at the cabin or the children, I guess she got the story from Katie.

The twenty-five-mile ride was filled with spurts of silence and forced chuckles.

She felt it too. I knew that. How could she not? Admittedly, the conversation did take an interesting turn when she asked me, "Do you think we'll ever have hot dogs again? I love hot dogs."

It was a weird comment, but talking food wasn't so bad. Food always seemed to breed comfort.

I knew it was going to be short lived, though. We turned on to the road towards the cabin, and that meant the time to deal with Fleck had arrived.

THREE

GAIN

Fleck

I always knew there was something off about Katie.

A five-year-old shouldn't handle the dead walking like she did. It didn't faze her. And while she placed on that fake, sympathetic, "I'm sorry" look, I knew the truth: she was loving it. The twisted little being that she was.

Katie and I had this strange relationship.

She picked on me.

Yeah, I was a grown ass man, and she was a psychic in a pint-size body, but she still picked on me. She'd draw demented drawings of my death, impending illnesses, what have you.

Her pessimistic drawings and predictions God damn freaked me out.

But when I saw the dark veins creeping up my body faster than I expected them to, I knew the small-bodied terror was the only one that could pull it off.

"Katie, I need you to tie me up," I said to her.

"Are we playing a game, Fleck?"

Did she really think we were playing a game? There were times I kept forgetting how young she was.

"No, Katie, we're not. I need you to make sure I am tied up. And tight."

"Where?" she asked.

"Excuse me?"

"Where do I tie you up?"

I thought about it. The small camper was out. Bella's body was still in there. Man, we did not have luck with campers at the cabin. I needed to be away from the kids, but close enough to hear if anything was wrong. Not that a tied-up Fleck could do anything, but at least I'd be able to yell while I still was in my right mind.

"Since I don't like him much, we'll lock me in Sean's room."

Katie giggled, then blurted out a playful, "Okay."

I had the stuff ready: duct tape, rope. That would be enough, I hoped. I didn't have any idea when Ben would be back, or Sean for that matter. They left to try to save Christian by taking him to The Colony, leaving me as babysitter.

I seriously didn't think twice about anything.

Until I had that intense itch. A nagging itch right above my right ankle bone. I thought maybe I got bit by something and when I lifted my pant and lowered my sock, I saw the veins.

My heart sunk.

I was willing to wager that they hadn't even arrived at The Colony yet.

How did it happen so fast? I mean, we scanned every morning. That was the question on my mind and then I thought about Bella.

She turned so fast, too fast, we just saw her an hour earlier and she was fine.

I couldn't take that chance.

What if that happened to me? What if in an instant I turned?

Every second, every minute that went by I grew more worried. I didn't care about myself, I really didn't, I worried about the kids. What happened if I turned in a snap and attacked them?

They were defenseless. My only choice was to take an offensive and make sure, to the best of my ability, that I couldn't and *wouldn't* get them.

I figured at the earliest, they would be back in ninety minutes.

"What's going on?" Sawyer asked when he saw me pulling a chair and a bunch of rope into the bedroom.

"Hey, guy, I need you to watch June while Katie helps me with something. You're the oldest," I told him. "You're gonna have to be in charge."

"Why?" he asked. "What are you going to be doing? Are you going somewhere?"

I didn't want to tell him I was locking myself in Sean's bedroom for fear of turning, because I didn't want to scare him. So, I said nothing.

"Are you sick? Do you have it?" Sawyer asked.

Man, these post apocalypse kids were perceptive.

"Sawyer…"

"You do. Don't we have a way for you to get to The Colony? They have a cure."

"I know."

"Fleck, you have to take the cure."

"I want to, bud, but how am I gonna get there? Until someone gets back, I have to make sure I don't turn and hurt you."

12

"So why are you having Katie help you and not me?" he asked.

Katie answered before I could. "Because I'm immune. You're not. Step back."

How did she know? I wondered. Another perceptive ward of the dystopian world?

Sawyer nodded. "I will. But Fleck, I don't think you'll turn. Sean or Pap will be right back, and they'll help you get to The Colony. You'll get that cure. You have to."

I saw it. That twinkle Katie got in her eye when she had that spooky intuition.

We went into the bedroom, and I sat down, immediately taping my legs to the chair.

"I'm not going to be able to do my hands. You'll have to do them. Use the duct tape, just like I'm gonna do with my legs."

I finished the ropes and handed the other two to her. Then I grabbed the tape.

"Okay." She smiled.

"You don't have to like it so much, Katie," I told her as I secured my legs. "I know you don't like me."

"I like you, Fleck, in fact I love you. It's just funny."

"How? How is this funny?" I handed her the tape.

"Because you're not gonna turn, silly." She started wrapping the rope around my wrists and I saw she didn't tie very well.

"Katie, you're gonna really have to put the tape on if you want it to hold."

"I will." She started humming. "I'll put lots on."

"Great."

"They'll have a hard time getting it off of you. They're on their way."

"Who?" I asked. "Ben and Sean?"

Rip.

Hum.

Katie drew up a sad look. "Ben is sick. He's not gonna die. But he's not coming. He's hurt."

"Are you sure?

She nodded.

Rip.

Hum.

"Do you really think I'm not gonna turn?" I asked.

I cringed; I was asking a child.

"You'll come close, but you won't turn."

"Gee. Thanks."

Rip.

Hum.

"Done." She looked at me.

I was secure. I even tried to get out, but it was pretty tight, and I felt better about that.

"Shut the door," I told her. "If you hear anything, if I turn, lock yourself in the other room. Okay?"

Katie nodded. "You'll be fine. I know it. You're not in the new drawing." Hands behind her back she headed to the door.

"New drawing?"

"Yeah." Then before she left, again, she looked sad. "There are people that need help, Fleck. Not now, but they will. It's in the drawing."

"What people, Katie?"

"I don't know," she said with a shrug, then closed the door and left.

There I was. Tied and bound with almost an entire roll of tape courtesy of Katie.

She left me confused, but I felt confident she left me secure enough that if I did turn, I couldn't get to the kids.

Hopefully, the pint-size terror was right, and help was on the way.

FOUR

REFLECTION

Nila

The rhythmic sound of the dueling heartbeats was like white noise. Combined with the mild sedative, I fell asleep to that sound and woke in a panic to utter silence.

I sat up in the bed with a start, only to see a woman removing the fetal heart monitors. I didn't know who she was, nor had I met her before.

"What's wrong?" I gasped. "What's wrong with the babies?"

When I came in with Ben, I was bleeding, the stress was a lot. I knew with twins pregnancy was high risk.

She smiled gently, placing her hand on my wrist. "Everything is fine. Doctor Rosen said we don't need to monitor anymore. Everything looks good."

Exhaling, I lay back, bringing my hand to my forehead. My heart raced out of control.

"Try to relax."

"Are they back yet?" I asked.

"I'm not sure what you mean."

"Almada."

She looked a bit confused. "I wasn't aware she went anywhere. Would you like me to get Doctor Rosen?"

16

"Could you please? Thank you."

I relaxed some, without a clue how long I had been sleeping or how long Sean and Almada had been gone. I was alone in the room, and that pretty much confirmed that they hadn't returned. Surely, if they had, Katie would be by my side.

"Nila." Doctor Rosen entered my room. "Are you alright?"

"Just nervous."

"The babies are fine."

"I know, but what about Almada and Sean? Any word?" I asked.

Rosen shook his head. "Not yet, they had to get things together before they left. I would guess they are there or arriving now. But there's been no radio contact."

"How's Ben?"

"Ben has the virus," Rosen stated. "No change either way. But Almada is confident the cure works. It worked on her."

I nodded.

"Nila, you can't stress yourself out, okay? I need you to try to remain calm, at least for a few hours. I know the loss of those in your group is hard, but for the sake of those babies, I need you to just rest."

The loss of those in my group.

Christian and Bella.

For a split second I had replaced the pain of those loses with worry about my babies, but that pain and guilt came flooding back in an instant.

"As soon as I hear anything, I will let you know. I'm sure it will be before we leave."

"You're leaving?" I asked almost in shock.

17

"My wife and I, yes. We're going back to our Colony."

"But you were convincing me to stay."

"I know, but we have to get back to our Colony, Nila. We're needed there."

"I understand, I do."

"Ben will be better soon, and you trust him, right?" Rosen asked. "He'll be with you as well. But I'll be back a couple times before those babies come. It's a big deal. If I could stay, I would, but I don't make the rules." He gave a sympathetic smile, and a gentle pat to my ankle, then turned and walked out.

He didn't make the rules.

I knew Almada had told me she wasn't in charge, in fact she used the words, "not even close." When we were at the other colony, I never bothered to find out who was in charge. Perhaps after things settled, before I made any final decisions, I needed to find out who ran all the colonies, and more importantly, what were the rules.

FIVE

REPLICATE

Sean

"June saved my life," I told Almada.

She had finally breeched the subject of family, pre-virus, and I told her that I lost my wife and son, but the most traumatic loss was my innocent daughter because I wasn't fast enough to get to her and save her. My torment and punishment was to witness what the dead did to her and relive that over and over.

Until June.

It was like a second life in a video game, nearly the same scenario, only I succeeded. I was able to get June before the dead got her. It didn't make up for my inability to save my own child, but June certainly gave me purpose again.

I saw what her father had done for her, at least I believed it was her father. June had to have been a baby when it all happened, and she was well taken care of. Someone loved her very much and I owed it to that person, as a father, to continue to take care of her.

It was a little crazy to wrap my head around it. But in a sense, I found a way to move on a little with life in a dead world."

I wanted to ask Almada, "What about you?"

I didn't.

19

I knew how painful it was to be asked that; if she wanted to tell me, she would.

"June is lucky to have you," she said.

"We're both lucky."

"What do you know about Finn McCaffrey?"

It took me a second to realize who she was asking about. "You mean Deacon McCaffrey?"

"I didn't realize that's what you called him."

"Well, that's how he introduced himself," I said. "He was a big church deacon when things fell apart, and he was head of council when Colony One still stood. Why do you ask?"

"So, you don't know him personally, friends, I mean?"

"No, not really."

Almada sighed out, stared toward the windshield for a moment then glanced at me.

"What?" I asked.

"Good, then I can trust you won't tell him about this when he makes an appearance in a couple days."

"Why is it a secret? I mean, you said those doses were for us if Katie gave her blood."

"I did." Almada nodded. "And I keep my word. But the doses are not to be used. By order of The Colony, and since he is now third in charge, I don't want it to get out."

"What are they gonna do?" I laughed. "Fire you?"

"Worse."

"*Kill* you?" I asked in disbelief.

"Maybe, or they'll just move me to a hot zone."

"Just say no. It's that simple."

"No, it's not. I want to beat this, and I will do it any way I can."

"How do you explain the missing vials and patients in quarantine?"

"Oh, the vials aren't missing. I have placebos there and will replace them one by one as I make more," she explained. "And only a select few know Ben's real condition. But I am worried about something else and that is why I wanted to take the ride with you to get the others."

"What is it?"

"Nila's baby."

"The immune one?" I asked.

Almada shook her head. "The infected one. I don't think he's infected; I think he is the true key to ending this. His amnio is just reading that, but there were markers in the DNA that told me otherwise. Markers Katie doesn't have."

I questioned. "Does Doctor Rosen know this?"

"Not yet. But it won't be long before another scientist does, and they'll test him when he's born."

"Okay." I really wasn't understanding where she was going.

"I'm fearful, Sean, of what they'll do with the baby when they find out what I want to confirm. I could go without confirming it, but if I don't someone else will."

My foot immediately went to hit the brake, as if a deer jumped out in the middle of that winding road. It was a shock to hear that from her. "Why did you push so hard to have her stay?"

"Because it was only eight hours ago we discovered this. I started working right away and then all that happened with Ben, Christian, Bella."

"So, you could be wrong."

"I could be wrong."

21

"If you're not?"

"Again, I'm afraid of what they'll do."

"Who?" I blurted out. "Who will do? I'm confused."

"The Council of the Colonies, which includes the best minds in their field. They won't kill the baby, but I can see them taking him in the name of science. Our best hope is they won't test it and when the baby remains alive in utero, they'll believe the initial testing saying he was infected was wrong."

"Jesus. I mean you pulled an attack on our camp to get Katie, what would they do to get someone they believed was the key?"

"I got her before anyone else could. But it's not going to be long before I am not in control of what happens with Katie and the new baby, and any promises I make will be worth squat."

"What do we do?" I asked. "We're pulling up to the cabin now. You think you could have started this conversation earlier?"

"I'm sorry. I have ideas. I'll discuss it with you all after we finish this and are with Nila. For the time being everything is safe. I'm still in control of what is getting done. That amnio hasn't gone farther than me. But the plan has to be decided as a group."

"If it's somewhere safe, what's the downfall?" I asked.

"It would mean going before the twins are born, and that is risky."

I inhaled deeply with concern and frustration, but I couldn't address that. We had pulled up to the gate and as soon as I stepped out to unlock it, I saw the kids, all three along with the two dogs. They were outside playing and laughing.

"What the hell?" I said, undoing the gate and flinging it open.

Almada stepped out of the SUV. "What's wrong?"

"Where's Fleck? Why are the kids out here playing alone? Bring in the SUV and lock the gate. I need to see what's going on." I took a few steps farther into the yard. The kids were oblivious and running around. "Sawyer!" I hollered to him as he ran with June. "Where's Fleck?"

"Inside."

"Great thanks." I walked toward the cabin. Katie ran by me, and I stopped her. "Katie, why are you guys out here alone. Where's Fleck?"

"Fleck's in the cabin."

"Is he getting something?"

"No, he has something," she replied.

"Why isn't he out here?"

"He's tied up."

"What is he so busy with that he is in there?"

"Huh?" she asked, confused.

"You said he was busy."

"I said he was tied up," she replied.

"Same difference."

Katie giggled. "I beg to differ."

"You...beg to differ? Beg to differ? It's the same unless..." the revelation hit me. "Unless he's really tied up."

Katie nodded. "With duct tape and rope."

"Who tied him up?"

"Me."

"Is it a game?"

"No, silly." She shook her head. "To be safe. He has the virus bad."

My eyes widened in horror, and I flew into the cabin.

SIX

MIRRORED

Fleck

The crowd chanted my name.

Fleck! Fleck! Fleck!

They were muffled, of course they were, I was trapped. It was the single moment every wrestler dreamt of.

Fleck! Fleck! Fleck!

A match with a legend.

I had wrestled in the independent circuit most of my adult life. Actually, the dead rising halted that career. For a short span of time, in my late twenties, I got a shot at the pros.

The big leagues. National television, all the drama and star power. I earned that shot, not just because I had been wrestling since I was fourteen, but because I did that reality television show, *Elimination*; best wrestler gets a contract.

I was the best. I won.

I got the contract, but the fame and glory…the main event never came to fruition. I became what was known as a wrestling jobber. Someone that is there to build up the main eventer and take the fall. One year later, my contract expired. I was still doing autograph sessions at conventions, but that went away.

The day I knew the world was over was the day my old ass was getting a second shot. I was wrestling down in Florida in a midsize league. I was the main event in a tag team title match, and a promoter from Japan was in attendance. I worried because, even though we talked it out, my partner and one of our opponents, Duffy, seemed off. He was the 'heel' of the other team, and an awesome wrestler; the crowd loved to hate him. But again, he was off. He looked a little pale, was sweaty and appeared to be coming down with something.

Little did I know, right?

I attributed his lack of energy to working too hard. He just flew in from Cleveland, where he wrestled in another league.

He downed an energy drink and perked up.

That was, until what was *supposed* to be the big finish. It was meant to be simple. After twenty-seven minutes of really good, crowd pumping moves, Duffy was to really go crazy on my partner, Joel. Joel would get away, tag me in. I'd clothesline Duffy, off the top rope for the pin.

Ding. Ding. Ding.

Fleck! Fleck! Fleck!

It didn't happen that way. I thought Joel accidentally broke Duffy's neck. In fact, I got worried when Joel did a drop kick, Duffy fell back and didn't move.

He didn't move at all.

In the business, after a minute, you worry that it isn't dramatics. To make sure, Joel kicked him, nudged him. Nothing.

I remember the look on Joel's face when he dropped down to check on Duffy, faking a pin and Duffy went nuts.

I was pissed, thinking he threw the plan out the window to showboat for the promoter, until I saw all the blood.

Duffy stood up, still grasping Joel, his mouth sunk into Joel's neck like a monster vampire, and he pulled away, ripping at the flesh.

Fleck! Fleck! Fleck!

The beginning of the end.

Or was it?

Because I was in another match. The crowds were chanting my name. Only I was trapped, tied up in that coffin and I had to break free before the Legend, Undertaker, lit the coffin on fire.

Fleck! Fleck! Fleck!

I was the baby face, the good guy. Tied up in there, I was still trying to figure out how I got there.

How did I suddenly earn this high-stakes match in the apocalypse? I went from keeper of kid mountain to Wrestle-Mania.

I drew all my rage, my anger, twisting and turning. My adrenaline built and I growled with each attempt to free myself. If didn't know better, I swore I broke my wrist freeing my hand from the tape and rope.

There were knocks and bumps on the coffin cover. But I still heard my name.

Moving back and forth, up and down, I kept trying to slam that chair to crack it.

Finally, I broke free, and it was at the same time, the coffin flung open.

Sean?

Why was it Sean and not the Undertaker? Dude, I'm in the middle of the match of a lifetime. Get away.

Then it hit me, right before Sean hit me, that I wasn't in a coffin. I wasn't in a professional match. The crowd wasn't chanting my name, it was Sean trying to get to me and I was turning.

I really never liked him but when I realized it was him, I was glad.

Muttering out a desperate "help me," was the last thing I remembered, and it was lights out.

SEVEN

NEW DAY

Nila

October 22

"Just stop," Ben told me. "You're not leaving forever. You'll be back."

I had been on bed rest for two weeks, and was halfway through my pregnancy, so now it was time to go back to the cabin, get what we needed, and return to The Colony until the babies were born.

I was glad Ben was better and had taken the trip to the cabin with me.

I got medical permission from Ben to do a salvage run; it was good to get out of the Alpha Colony and be on the road. I needed it more than I'd realized.

The day was still young and once we dropped off the items at The Colony, I was hitting the road. It would be fun to go back out with Fleck. I knew since he'd gotten the cure and snapped back to his old self, that he'd been non-stop, getting our new, temporary home ready.

Which I knew I was going to hate. Not that Fleck wasn't doing a good job, I was sure he was doing his best to make it great for us, but it wasn't the cabin. It wasn't home.

There would be zero visual reminders of Lev.

My mind was healing over the emotional trauma of Bella and Christian, but it was far from healed over my loss of Lev.

One more look at the cabin. One more glance to the porch where he took his last breath.

It was so hard to walk away. I locked the doors, as if that would convince my mind that I was closing that chapter, and yet I still looked back every ten feet I walked away from it.

"If I have to hold your head and make you face forward, I will," Ben said.

"I know. I know." I inhaled. "Last look." I turned my head.

"Nila."

"I'm done."

Really, I wasn't, but Ben wouldn't let me live it down. I was being ridiculous and the more I looked back, the more my neurotic mind kept thinking something was going to happen, and that some sort of burning psychic instinct was telling me it was the last time I would look at the cabin.

Finally, we got in the car to head back to The Colony.

I reached over and cranked the heat.

"It's not even that cold."

"Maybe it's the babies."

"They should act like a furnace," Ben told me.

"I know, right. Weird. Maybe because they kept my hospital room at a thousand degrees."

"Then maybe it is good you get out today," Ben said. "Just no picking on Fleck."

"Picking on Fleck?" I laughed. "You cannot be serious. How do I pick on Fleck? Katie does. Not me."

"Nila, ever since he mentioned his fever hallucination, you…"

I couldn't help it. Thinking about Fleck believing he was in a coffin match with the Undertaker just cracked me up.

"You do that."

"Ben, it's funny."

"I know. But he was scared, and Nila, he was close to turning."

I waved out my hand. "Oh, he was fine."

"He was not."

"Ben, the serum reversed that virus within a day. It took you nearly a week."

"I was bit, Nila," Ben said.

"And yeah, you tell me not to pick on Fleck when he makes fun of your disability now."

"My missing ear is not a disability, it's a cosmetic annoyance."

"That's funny," I said. "Why don't you come out with us? The Colony cleared most of the deaders from Evans City, we can stop by the *Night of the Living Dead* Museum."

Ben just glanced at me sideways. "I'll pass."

"Your son loved it."

"Cade was weird like that," Ben said. "I mean you and him took all those pictures. Which, I am forever grateful for."

"Yeah, me, too. Which reminds me." I snapped my finger. "I need to get more ink."

"You have more pictures?"

"I do. I'm hoping there's more photos of Lev, but he never liked getting his picture taken."

Ben chuckled. "You took the one of him when he was all banged up."

"No, that was Katie," I corrected. "So, what's our new place look like? I asked Katie and she didn't really say."

"Like a section of a school converted into an apartment. A big apartment, nonetheless."

"Why do they have everyone living in the schools?" I shook my head. "High school, middle school, grade school."

"The higher ups get the Presbyterian preschool down the road."

"Why?"

"Because they can keep people safe this way. But they got some shops opened up."

I grumbled. "I get the return to normalcy, but, until this thing is cured, a vaccine is made, and the deaders are, well, dead and gone, there will be no normalcy. I just hope they don't do the plan about gathering up all the young."

Ben shook his head with a scoffing face. "I highly doubt that. That was just an idea tossed about by the council."

"If I wasn't on bed rest, imprisoned in that room, I would have gone."

"I filled you in, you didn't miss a thing."

But I did.

At times I felt like they were intentionally keeping me away. But I understood, they had to keep an eye on the babies, especially Baby Lev, the twin suspected of being infected.

If he really had the virus in him, he would have passed in utero. But he didn't. Like his father he was strong, and they hadn't repeated an amnio. Which surprised me; if they were wrong about Baby Lev's infection, they could be wrong about Baby Earl's immunity too.

For the brief time I was out of that medical bay, it felt good. But there I was back again in the next building, the main one. Ben truly overstated it when he said it looked like a school converted into an apartment. Maybe I was just being harsh, but stepping in classroom 6A reiterated that as soon as the babies were born, I was headed back to the cabin.

It was a large classroom with modular panel wall kits set up to create rooms. They had an accordion style door on them. They were bad, but it was still a classroom.

I put on a smile because Fleck looked so proud.

"Nice job," Ben told him.

"Thanks." Fleck grinned. "It's a converted Home Ec room so the kitchen is nice. I tried to decorate a bit. Hit some of the houses out there, got furniture that didn't have a deader stain, goo, or smell." He waved out his hand. "Living room, kitchen, and it's an open concept."

He walked over to the modular walls. "First room is for you and Katie. Other is Ben and Sawyer. Right now, they're like government issued FEMA beds, but it's temporary, right?"

Ben asked. "Bathroom?"

"Right next to your room," Fleck replied. "Ben, they are sweet ass modular bathrooms. They're small like a cruise ship but they work."

"Wait. Wait." I held up my hand. "Where are Sean and June and you? Are you three living together?"

Fleck laughed hysterically. Loud and forced then quickly stopped. "No. I'm not living with Sean and his adopted toddler. He's 6B that's right next door, and I'm one floor below you. You can stomp and I'll hear you."

"Why?" I asked. "Why are we not all living together? It's the apocalypse, it's the not the time to seek independence."

"I'm in the same building. We talked about space, Nila," Fleck stated. "You know, we even went camper shopping, but we don't have luck with those. Besides, I didn't think you liked living with me that much."

"I don't, but still."

Ben shook his head. "He needs space, Nila, away from the kids."

"Does Sean know?" I asked.

"Oh, yeah, he and June have been next door for a week. Their place was already done."

"He didn't say anything to me."

"Nila," Ben said calmly. "Why is this a big deal?"

"Because we left my home, and even if I don't like living with some people." My eyes shifted to Fleck. "All of you are family. You're home."

Fleck stepped to me. "I'm not far. I promise you'll see me all the time. Like today, are we not going out and doing our thing?"

"We are." I nodded. "And please know, your efforts to *undertake*..." I emphasized the word snidely. "Are not unnoticed."

Fleck rolled his eyes. "I get the dig. Funny. Ha ha."

"I'm sincere. Thank you. Except..." I turned to the painting on the one modular wall. It looked like something from the seventies. A mountain scene with a woman in a long dress picking flowers. "This." I pointed to it. "Is this a joke?"

"No," Fleck balked. "What's wrong with the painting?"

"It's weird."

"Marsha picked it out," Fleck said. "She has good taste."

I started to chuckle, then turned curiously serious. "Who's Marsha?"

EIGHT

SAME DAY

Sean

It wasn't her heavy accent, that was for sure. I think it was the way her voice got really high on her vowels that slightly irritated me.

And she talked.

Boy, did Fleck's new friend talk, and we weren't even in the SUV yet.

"Hey, Sean, do you mind if Marsha comes?" Fleck asked me. "She would love to see Evans City. Big *Night of the Living Dead* fan."

"Have I met her?" I asked.

"No, but she's been helping me with the apartment."

"Did you ask Nila? This is her big day out."

"Ask me what?" Nila approached.

"If my friend Marsha can come along," Fleck said.

Nila shrugged. "Sure. You gotta be responsible for her though. Let me run back to Home Ec for some snacks and I'll meet you out there. Can't wait to meet the woman that picked out that painting. You should have her pick one out for Sean's place since, you know, he won't be around to see ours." She turned and walked away.

Fleck whistled.

"What?" I asked.

"Nothing."

"Whatever. Go tell your friend we're leaving."

"Oh, she's probably already out there."

And she was.

Her light brown hair was in a tight ponytail, and she wore one of those head bands as well. An older rifle was strapped over her shoulder, and she had a tough girl build, slightly hippy, as if she could kick some ass if need be. When Fleck introduced us, she greeted me with a firm handshake. I knew right then, by how she made eye contact, she was a good person and I was going to like her.

"Nice to meet you. Sean, you say?" she asked in her thick obvious, Minnesota accent. "I think Fleck told me all about you."

"Really?" I asked in disbelief. "If Fleck was saying it, it can't be good."

"Oh. You know Fleck. Always joking. He's a card."

"Yeah, he is. Hmm. So, what part of Minnesota are you from?"

She grinned. "How'd ya know? The accent?"

"And the fact that you're wearing a wind breaker and it's thirty-four degrees out."

"Oh, it's still warm." She flung out her hand. "Sun is out. It's gonna be a nice day. I'm so glad Fleckie invited me."

I mouthed the word, 'Fleckie?' shifting my eyes to Fleck who seemed unfazed.

"Yeah, good thing," I said. "So, how'd you end up here in this Colony?"

"My dad. He travels back and forth here. I thought I'd stay for a while."

Fleck explained, "Her father is Doctor Rosen, Nila's baby doctor."

My eyes widened with surprise. "Oh, wow, that's cool. So, Gwen ..."

"Is not my mom." She shook her head. "Stepmother. Nice woman. My mom is the original OG wife."

What's an OG wife?

"I see, well, let me go rush Nila. I wanna get on the road. What is taking her so long to grab snacks?"

"Here she comes," Fleck said.

"Probably was talking to him," Marsha added. "Isn't he just a bushel of handsome? I'd dally too. Not to get you jealous, Fleckie."

"No jealousy here," Fleck replied.

I turned to see who the 'bushel of handsome' was and it turned out, Nila was smiling and walking with Deacon McCaffrey. I never noticed his 'handsomeness,' to me he was just some ass in charge that I didn't like.

"We're ready to roll, Nila," I said.

"I'm sorry, we were talking. Do you know Finn?" she asked.

McCaffrey replied, "We do. We worked together at the other colony." He shook my hand. "Sean. Maybe next time I can come along."

"Maybe."

He faced Marsha. "Good to see you."

"Good to see you, too, Finn," she replied and darted a kiss to his cheek.

"Fleck." He shook his hand as well.

"Seems I am the only one that didn't know you, Finn," Nila said.

"Now you do."

"Are you sure you don't want to come?" Nila asked him.

Please say no. Please say no, I thought.

"I can't," he said.

Whew. Thank God.

"I'll see you later," he said.

"Sounds good." Nila smiled.

McCaffrey backed up from the SUV, pointing as he did. "Watch them babies."

"What are you seeing him later for?" I asked Nila.

"Talk. Hang out." She shrugged.

"Why?"

"What does it matter?" she replied. "He's a nice guy."

"No, Nila he's not." I turned my head when I heard Masha gasped sharply. "What? Bushels of Handsome isn't a dick?"

Again, she gasped with a scolding look, then dropped her voice to a whisper as she got into the SUV. "You were absolutely spot on about him," she told Fleck while looking at me.

"See. I told you." Fleck shut the door for her, gave me a shitty grin, then walked around to the other side.

I felt the tap to my chest and looked down.

"Ignore him. Get in the SUV," Nila said. "You can tell me about Bushels of Handsome in Evans City."

I nodded, implying that I would, but somehow putting a damper on the day by stating my mistrust and dislike of Deacon McCaffrey didn't seem quite right. Even though I knew he was only getting close to Nila for those babies.

Dissing on the deacon wasn't what the day was supposed to be about.

My feelings could wait. After all, he wasn't going to be around all that much and at the moment we had more important, annoying things to deal with like Fleck and his perky new friend.

NINE

DEAD DAY

Fleck

The moment that she called me Fleckie, I knew she was the one. Instantaneously, Marsha was the woman for me. Bonus. She even got along with Nila. Or rather, in a rarity, Nila got along with her.

Seeing them step out of the SUV after we pulled into Evans City was awesome. Both carrying a weapon: Nila with her utility weapon belt that now sat below her growing belly, and Marsha with her rifle. Both ladies looked ready to take on the dead, and win.

And there were plenty.

Admittedly, it was almost nice to see them. It had been a while, and a part of me wondered if they were still around.

Evans City deaders weren't a threat or fresh by any means. In fact, I'd guess it was a matter of weeks before they became sloshing bits of flesh moving on the ground, then finally nothing.

Since the weather was cooling, they had maybe a month left.

Evans City was almost done. It would be a safe zone before long.

Eventually, it would have to stop.

I mean, scientifically, it couldn't be a *Walking Dead* world where a zombie remains forever, that's not biologically possible.

The reason for me that it was still going on was this was the new strain of virus.

You didn't need to get bit to turn and that was scary.

"So where are we going?" Sean asked. "I know you want to go to this *Night of the Living Dead* Museum, if it's still standing."

"It is," Nila said, pretty sure of herself. "Me and Cade really blocked it off for future visits. I want to hit the Walgreens."

"Isn't there an apothecary?" Sean questioned. "You said something about it."

"Yeah, but that was picked through a year ago," Nila replied. "Walgreens is about four blocks down."

"Are we walking?" Sean asked.

I laughed once. "Dude, we don't need to drive. I know there's a lot of deaders, but they can barely move. They're the gross ones."

"Yeah," Nila agreed. "Don't touch them, your hand will sink right in."

"Gotcha," Marsha said. "So, we aren't shooting them either?"

I shook my head. "We can walk by them, knock them down, but in case there's any fresh ones, we don't want to make the noise to attract attention."

Then Sean made the comment, "Not that the rifle is gonna do you any good. What? It's a .22? Hunting rifle from a sporting goods store?"

"Dude," I snapped. "Be nice."

"Just saying."

"Oh, he doesn't offend me." Marsha flung out her hand. "But by the way, mister, I got this at Walmart when I was fifteen." She grinned at Sean. "And you betcha this thing will work. Remember, like any *weapon*, it's not the size or type, but how you use it." She winked, laughing to herself as she walked ahead to join Nila.

Sean turned to me, somewhat shocked. "Did she just compare a rifle to a...a...*penis?!*"

"Yeah." I grinned. "What a girl. Don't get any ideas."

"What do you mean?" Sean asked.

"Hitting on her."

"I wouldn't dream of it."

"I know you've moved on from Nila," I said.

"What are you talking about, 'moving on from Nila'?"

"You got your own place."

"Because you wouldn't stop fighting with me."

"Ha," I scoffed. "I don't even live there, and you still moved out."

"Before I knew you weren't gonna live there."

"It's Almada, huh? You got a thing for her," I said.

"I don't have a thing for Almada."

"So, it's still Nila. She's never getting over Lev."

"I don't have a thing for Nila," Sean snapped.

"It's Marsha then."

"You're an idiot. Not everyone wants to find love in the apocalypse."

"Guys." Nila turned around using that scolding mother voice. "Can you two just stop. Please. I just can't...Fleck. Shit. Watch out." She reached for her utility belt.

Stop.

42

I thought she was warning me that Sean was going to hit me, after all what else would it be? But why wasn't she warning Sean?

Probably because she saw that deader raging toward me. I never saw him or smelled him until he was on top of me.

It happened so fast. He came from my right; I caught a quick view of him from the corner of my eye. He was strong, fast, and he didn't smell, which told me that he was fresh.

Trying to do my best wrestling move, I attempted to flip him when he came for my shoulder. But he grabbed hold of my hoodie, and if I threw him, I knew I was going down with him. When he moved his grip to my arm, I was able to turn fast enough to face him and push him away.

He wasn't bit; he had the virus and had turned.

The black veins crawled up his neck and over his face. I could tell he turned fast, too, because he was still wearing a small backpack. It looked full, and it gave him more weight that caused him to spin and fall toward the sidewalk space before me. He toppled to his knees, catching himself before he fell completely, and he quickly jumped back up.

By then I had my hammer in my hand ready to go, when I heard the shot fired.

A single shot.

I hesitated.

A shot was fired. Surely, the deader with the blue backpack was going down. But he didn't. He raged toward me. This time I was ready. I swung out hard and with his momentum, I landed the hammer to the side of his head. Of course, he was fresh, the skull was still hard, and it only paused him. It was enough of a pause for me to gain my momentum and strike him three more times before he went down.

I heard enthusiastic applauding when that happened. I glanced up, Marsha was grinning.

"Nice job, Fleckie!" she said proudly.

"Thanks." Then I looked at Nila. "You okay?"

"Yeah, why?" Nila replied.

"You shot and you missed. You never miss," I said.

"I didn't shoot," Nila said then pointed to Marsha.

"You shot?" I asked.

"I did," she said perkily, then winced. "But I missed."

Then I heard Sean speak up, his tone steely. "No," he said. "She didn't miss."

"Huh?" I was confused and looked to the deader.

"Oh, shit," Nila stepped over the deader and hurried to Sean. "He's hit."

TEN

THROUGH THE WINDOW

Nila

Being a woman in a deader filled world is not without its challenges. They aren't physical or even emotional, they are men. Somewhere in the unwritten rulebook of the world, men suddenly believed they had to take on the alpha male rule.

I was sure Sean wasn't an alpha male before the virus, Fleck, maybe, not Sean.

Yet, there they both were bickering at each other in a verbal pissing contest of sorts.

They probably would have bickered on the street had Marsha's Walmart rifle not alerted three deaders to our presence. New deaders who were still in that raging stage. It was hard to tell if they had turned and raged, or died and raged. There were those, like Bella, that didn't need to die first to become a monster.

It would have been easy to take them out, but who knew how many more were out there?

Evans City, according to Almada, was a finished town. No real deader threats. So where did the fresh ones come from? My guess: the one that attacked Fleck was with a group that was traveling together, got the virus together, and turned together.

With there possibly being more, we needed to focus on Sean's gunshot wound. Marsha hit him in the left leg, just below the knee. While it didn't seem life threatening, Sean was bleeding, and we needed to make sure it wasn't more serious.

Oddly enough, the first place to run to was the same apothecary that Cade and I had stopped at, where he was bit by the deader on the ground. In fact, that same deader was still there and now a mere pile of crumbling bones. I was stuck in that moment, my eyes locked on the dusty bottle of Bactine right where I had left it that day with Cade.

"Oh!" Marsha said cheerfully. "Wonderful, medical supplies." She grabbed the Bactine. "I found some bandages; I'll go look for more stuff."

"Just something to stop the bleeding," Sean called out to her. "Then we have to clear the dead and get back. The shell is in my calf muscle, I feel it. A little help here, Fleck? Nila?"

I turned around and saw him sitting on an overturned shelf. "Sorry." I winced. "I was kinda caught up. This was where Cade and I stopped for stuff."

Fleck said, "And here I thought you were being sentimental over the Bactine."

"Why would you say that?" I asked.

"You let out an 'ah' when you saw it, like it meant something."

"It kind of did," I replied. "Okay. I have water, we can clean the wound, but if I'm not mistaken there is still a bunch of first aid stuff here." I walked over to Sean. "Marsha is checking now."

Sean lifted his pant leg. "I can't believe this happened."

"It was an accident," Fleck replied. "She missed."

"Missed. The deader was five feet in front of her, I was ten feet to her right."

Fleck shrugged. "Not everyone is a sharpshooter."

"What happened to the insinuation that she was a good shooter?" Sean asked. "You know the 'rifle is a penis' sex reference?"

"Dude." Fleck winced. "Ladies are present. Does it hurt?"

"Not that bad. Just bleeding."

"Keep pressure on it," Fleck said.

"I am," Sean replied.

"Here." Marsha raced over. "Use this until we get the medical supplies together."

I saw the look on Sean's face when he realized what she extended to him. He looked at it and then her. "Are you serious? That is feminine protection."

"It's a pad," she corrected.

I watched both my alpha males cringe and that made me laugh.

"Don't worry," Marsha told Sean. "I got you."

"So, you're good with medical stuff?"

She smiled, chuckled, then shook her head. "No. Not really but maybe. I was in the girl scouts, but more importantly my father is a doctor."

"Is that like saying you're not a doctor but you play one on TV?" Sean asked.

Again, Marsha giggled. "Now, hold still. I'll get this sucker cleaned and try to stop bleeding."

"With a pad?" asked Sean.

"Oh, yeah and duct tape." She held up the duct tape then lifted the Bactine.

Sean reached out and stopped her. "Did you get that here?"

She nodded.

"Marsha, that has to be expired and I really wish you wouldn't..."

She squirted four times quickly.

"Spray," Sean finished, then...screamed. "What the hell?"

"Sorry." She proceeded to blow on his wound.

'Are you blowing on me?" Sean asked.

"To stop the stinging."

Fleck shook his head. "I really hope Sean doesn't throw out another sexual reference again."

I found the whole thing amusing. Marsha put the pad on Sean's leg, told him to hold it and he said he'd rather not touch it, so I walked over.

I held it firmly in place while Marsha secured it with duct tape. Which was actually a really good idea.

"There." Marsha stood. "All better."

"No, it's not," Sean griped.

I gave an approving smile to Marsha, and then when she moved, I stood before Sean. "Can you stop?"

"Stop what?" he asked.

"Being so mean. She's trying."

"She *shot* me."

"It was an accident. She didn't know Walmart rifles fire forty-five degrees off to the right."

"No, they don't." Sean staggered to a stand. "Don't tell her that either." He hobbled over to the window. "We have those two out there and if we can get rid of them, the rest are not a threat."

"You cannot make it two blocks to the car, not fast," I said. "And we'll have to be fast."

Fleck spoke up and pointed. "I can put him in the shopping cart."

Sure enough, Fleck pointed to a grocery cart inside the store.

"No," Sean said. "You are not putting me in a cart."

"You'll fit," replied Fleck. "I'll push you, and it's really the only way to get to the car fast enough."

"Oh," I perked up and lifted a backpack. "Can you put this in the shopping cart with you?"

Sean looked at it. "Where did that come from?'

"I took it from the deader Marsha missed. I figured we'd see what we can learn about them."

Marsha reached for it. "Here, I'll take it. I'll put it in the cart for you."

"Thanks."

Sean waved out his hand. "I never said I would ride in a shopping cart."

"Tough," I told him. "We're making a run for it."

"And I don't have a choice?"

"Not if you want to get back to The Colony fast," I said. "End of discussion. Marsha, help him in the cart. Fleck and I will take out the two fresh ones." I turned to Fleck. "Draw them away?"

Fleck stared out the window directly at one of the two deaders. They had turned no more than a week earlier; both were still in that fast-moving, rage phase. One was a man, the other a woman, neither of them had bites.

They tried diligently to get Fleck through the glass. Biting his bottom lip, Fleck turned around. "There's about eight of them out there, not including Rick and Rene rager. We can't draw them. The others are slow. Stage four decay."

Wow, there was a term I hadn't heard in a while.

Stage four decay or decomposition. It was something Ben and Lev came up with. And shared with the first Colony we went to. It was something we should have used more but didn't.

Ben determined there were five stages.

Stage one was either freshly dead and raging, or raging without death. Neither decayed the deader.

Each sequential stage brought more decay, slower movements and less threat. Stage two, they were dead but still moved fast and weren't as decomposed. Stage three they start to slow down, decay more.

Stage four was a point where it didn't take much to take them down. A simple hit would collapse the biological aspect of their bodies.

Stage five was like the dead in the pool house and the one on the floor that bit Cade. Decayed and rotted to the point they didn't move, and all that was left was the ability to snap a jaw. They were mere moments from being done.

So, a street full of stage four decays wasn't an issue, the two fresh ones were, along with the question of whether there were more.

"What then?" I asked Fleck.

"I think we prep the shopping cart, get ready to roll, take the fresh two out, pop, pop, and run for it. It's two blocks."

"The shots could attract more," I said. "Why don't we go out and take them out quietly?"

"I can't safely take out two ragers," Fleck said. "And you should not be doing any hand to hand." He handed me the rifle. "When I say go, you take them out. And we run for it."

I took the rifle. "Sounds like a plan. There doesn't look like many."

"Nah," Fleck said. "We've faced more. Okay." He clapped his hands and exhaled. "Let's do this." He walked a few feet toward the entrance, grabbed the shopping cart and pushed it toward Sean. "My man, your chariot awaits."

ELEVEN

THROUGH THE ORDEAL

Sean

Despite my best efforts there has never been any love lost between me and Fleck. None. I tried, probably more than he did. No, scratch that. He never tried. Fleck treated me like an enemy and someone that was always up to something.

Despite the way he was with me, I was still mostly cordial. Not anymore.

Those days were done, and Fleck would never be a friend to me. I was finished with him, and in my mind, there was nothing he could ever do that would make me like him.

I totally understood placing me in the shopping cart, I got it. I was injured and there was no way I could keep up. Heck, I even understood him moving fast. But to use me in the cart as some sort of plow to push any deader that came our way…that was too much.

He zig-zagged as we sped through the streets, and even went out of his way to hit some.

I honestly didn't think he'd do that.

We all waited by the door, except Nila. She stood a few feet from us, not much, eyes on the two fresh deaders that were causing the most commotion.

She was the best one to take them out because Nila was the best shot by far.

Marsha was by the door to open it.

Fleck had both hands on the cart.

I was in that cart, feet toward the end, and Nila raised her weapon.

The second Fleck shouted "GO" it went as planned.

Nila fired two consecutive shots, I doubted she missed, and we barreled out the door.

The slow-moving deaders at first moved toward the shots.

As we raced toward the SUV, I saw the deaders, only several, dragging ass, moving slow.

There was no reason whatsoever to aim for them.

Fleck did.

I yelled at him as he did it.

He claimed, "If I don't knock them down now, they'll come for the car while we're putting you inside."

Just a slight point, but still, we got me in the car pretty quickly. Those deaders didn't move fast and there weren't any more fresh ones.

Once inside I called him an asshole, and he laughed.

I was happy when we arrived at The Colony, and I was placed immediately in the medical unit.

"Do you want me to stay with you?" Nila asked.

"No, just go check on June for me please."

"Okay, I'll come back."

"No, I'm okay."

"Sean," she said gently. "I'm sorry. I am. I know you're in pain."

"I'm too angry to be in pain. Fleck did not need to hit every deader with the cart."

"I know. I'll talk to him."

"Don't bother," I said.

"Okay."

Quickly I looked at her. "Okay? Just, okay?"

"Well, what do you want me to say? Argue with you? Nope. I'll talk to him. Just after he's done being mad."

"What?" the question squeaked out. "What does he have to be mad at?"

"Him and Marsha are a little mad that you got injured and they didn't get to see the *Night of the Living Dead* Museum.'

"Are you kidding me? Are you really serious? I got shot because his new friend can't fire her Walmart rifle," I argued. "And they're mad at me?"

"No. I'm teasing."

"Oh my God." I sat back. "You're not helping."

"I'll go check on June and the kids."

I nodded.

"Are you sure you'll be okay?" she asked.

"I'll be fine. I'll just wait for the doctor here with a pad duct taped to my leg while an expired, bacteria infested massive amount of Bactine pushes me toward amputation."

She laughed.

"That's funny."

"Yeah, that is. I'm sure it's fine."

"I'm sure it's not."

And, in the midst of my irritable argumentative state, there was a knock on the door and a man entered.

"Hi, Sean? I'm Doctor Peters, I hear we have a bullet wound."

"And on that," Nila said. "I'm out. I'll let you get treated. I'll check back."

Doctor Peters smiled at her, then after she left, stepped closer to me. "That's the twin lady, huh?"

"That's her."

"I thought she was a myth." Doctor Peters shrugged. "Okay, you were shot. How did that happen?"

"It was an accident. The woman shooting missed."

"No, she didn't."

I chuckled a little. "You're right. It was a .22. The shell is whole. It's in there, you can see it, I just couldn't reach it."

"A maxi pad and duct tape." He rubbed his chin.

"I know."

"That's brilliant. Whoever thought of that, totally brilliant use of supplies." He reached for the scissors. "Did you clean the wound?"

"Rinsed it with water," I replied, watching him cut the tape. "But they put Bactine on it."

"Bactine? That has no medicinal value."

"I know. And it was old and expired."

"Yikes. Hopefully, it didn't have an opposite effect." He lifted the pad. "Well, I stand corrected."

"On?" I asked.

"Apparently, Bactine does have medicinal value, this looks good. Really good. You need to thank whoever was your medic in the field." He peered closer. "Oh, yeah, I see it. Shouldn't be difficult." He set down the makeshift bandage. "Alright, I'll leave you be, and I'll start prepping for surgery. Should be fast and easy. You're a lucky man. It could have been much worse, and they got you in here before it was."

I thanked him and realized he was right: it could have been worse.

While waiting for my surgery, I rethought my bad mood. It wasn't the time or place to remain angry and miserable. I promised myself I would be grown up about it, let it go, and move on. Of course, those inner promises didn't include Fleck.

Him? My grudge was lasting forever.

TWELVE

THROUGH THE RINGER

Fleck

Ben looked off. Probably a little irritated. I don't blame him, after all, he was kind of stuck with the kids, and we were going on our day out. Plus, I promised him a souvenir from the *Night of the Living Dead* Museum, which we failed to deliver.

I stopped by their little home economics apartment after making sure Sean was taken care of. Ben was helping Sawyer with schoolwork at the kitchen table, while June napped on the couch.

"You okay?" I asked him.

"Yeah, just a bit perturbed."

"You look it. Sawyer not getting the hang of the math problems?"

Sawyer looked at me. "I can do math."

"It's not Sawyer," Ben said. "Just…" He grunted. "I'm our family's doctor, you know. Why was I not called down when Sean was brought in for the gunshot?"

"Maybe because he needs surgery."

"I'm a surgeon."

I laughed. "Ben, no offense but you're a plastic surgeon. Sean doesn't need his eyes done."

"You're an asshole, Fleck, I wasn't always a plastic surgeon. I was a general surgeon in emergency medicine first."

"Oh well maybe you need to apply."

"Apply?" he asked.

Perhaps I wasn't being clear. "Apply. Not like apply yourself, more like apply for a job."

"I don't think I have to apply to be a doctor when I'm a doctor."

"You had to apply in the old world. Show your degrees. Just because it's the apocalypse doesn't mean you don't have to follow rules."

Sawyer shook his head as he worked on his schoolwork. "Why do you bother arguing with him, Pap?"

"You're right. What can I help you with, Fleck?"

"I just came by to check on everyone. Where's Katie? I'm headed down to play with Three Sixteen, thought she'd want to see her dog."

"She would love that. This whole thing has made her sad."

"I'll go tell her."

It wasn't far from the kitchen table to walk to the bedroom portions. The accordion door was open, and Katie was belly down on the floor with her crayons and sketchbook.

I knocked on the doorframe to alert her then spoke out. "Hey."

Katie's hands meticulously worked a drawing. She glanced over her shoulder at me. "Hello."

"You look like you're working pretty hard on that."

"I am," she replied. "It's gonna be a whole story. Pictures only."

"My kind of book." I nodded.

Katie giggled.

"I just got back from Medical. Sean's gonna be okay."

"I know."

"Of course, you do. Where'd you get the cool art supplies?"

"Almada. She's nice like that."

"Yeah, and Sean likes her," I said.

"I like her, too."

"Yeah, but you don't want to marry her. Sean does."

Again, Katie giggled.

"That is funny," I said. "I know."

"No." Katie shook her head. "I'm laughing because you're silly. Almie likes girls. Maybe she'll marry Mommy."

"That would be interesting. Anyhow." I clapped my hands together once. "Get your jacket and shoes. Let's go."

"Where are we going?"

"Dog time."

"Yes!" Katie dropped those crayons and jumped to her feet. "I'll be ready so fast. Thank you."

"You're welcome. Need to see our dogs."

While she got ready, I took the opportunity to take a peek at what she was working on, figuring it was more than likely something demented. But it wasn't. It was a drawing of a little girl holding a flower, oddly enough in what looked like snow.

I flipped back to see the ones she had drawn prior to that, and they too were pleasant and happy. There was a family. A man, a woman, the flower girl, and a taller boy.

The only picture I saw that wasn't pleasant was of a brown truck, wrecked, with blood covering the side of the road.

Strange, but Katie always liked to add blood. I was convinced she just liked red.

"Katie, wow, these are good. Look at the detail," I commented about the one of a house. A family stood out front, trees in the back and on top of those she'd drawn in the background; way in the back it looked like a motor oil sign, with a sun on it. "You even have a Sun Beam gas station sign way in the back. Like the tall ones from the highway."

"Yep. It's a big sign way in the back, they're high on a hill. They can see it. Like we would see the signs when we went to Big Bear, but that was McDonald's. I'm ready."

"Let's go. And these are really nice. It looks like a nice story."

Katie smiled before darting out the door. "It's not done yet. I'll be in it."

I didn't think much of her comment; she was creating a story and of course, she'd write herself into it.

There'd probably be a deranged twist where she killed the characters on the pages of her story, I would expect no less, after all it was Katie.

A girl and her dog.

It was a good decision to take Katie to the dog room. That was the one thing I hated about The Colony. While living in the building, we couldn't have our pets. It wasn't like they were in a pen or kennel, which was a good thing, I supposed. Instead, there were four people that kept them for us at one of the trailers on the property.

I wanted my dog back and I was sure Katie did too. So hopefully we'd move out of that building or somewhere else after Nila had the babies.

Three-Sixteen greeted me happily, and Caesar was ecstatic to see Katie. We went every day for the two weeks we were there. Well, not me. I had those few days when I was almost a deader.

While I played with my dog, I watched Katie and hers. How she drilled Max, the man watching our pets, about how many times he pets the dog and shows him love.

She giggled and laughed; it was fun to watch. Too bad I wasn't a big fan of kids.

"Fleck." Katie approached me. "Look. He has a collar and leash now. Max said when I have him out here, I have to keep him on a leash."

"Yeah, even though we know he's good, others don't."

"But I told Max he smells the dead."

"A good skill, too, but they probably don't believe you."

Katie grimaced and nodded. "Yeah. I don't like him being cooped up."

"Me either. Both these dogs are used to running," I said. "And the woods…"

"Do you think they get lost in the woods?" she asked.

"I don't know. Maybe. Maybe not. Dogs have a good sense of direction." I shrugged. "I think."

"Do dogs get cold, Fleck?"

"Yeah, they shiver," I replied.

"Can they walk in the snow?" she asked.

"Some dogs love the snow."

"Can they walk in the snow and not get freezing?"

"For a little while."

"How far can they walk? Should they be trained?"

"To walk in the cold?" I shook my head. "No. Katie, what's with all these weird questions?"

"Nothing." She shrugged. "Just curious." And then she ran off.

Shaking my head, I reached down to Three-Sixteen and pet him, sighing out. "She is such a strange kid."

THIRTEEN

ADJUSTING

Nila

Word came from Almada that Sean was awake and out of
recovery. I thought it would be nice to go visit him, to keep
him company for a little bit before relieving Ben of child
watching duties, so he could go to bed. Ben was tired and
the kids were pretty energetic.

I peeked in Sean's hospital room before knocking on the
open door. It was the same room I had been in for two
weeks. Surprisingly, he had the shades closed, so he wasn't
seeing the great view.

Instead, he was reading a book as he lay on the bed. His
leg was elevated and in a brace.

"Hey," I called out. "Feeling up for a visitor?"

He set down the book. "Absolutely."

"I brought you food." I placed the bag on the nightstand.
"And I thought we could go through *this*." I removed the
backpack from my shoulder.

"Is that from the deader that Marsha tried to shoot?" he
asked.

"Yep. Heavy too." I placed it on the floor. "Must have
been important because he never took it off when he got
sick."

"He probably turned fast."

"Probably." Before sitting down, I opened the bag of food to pull it out.

"So, you haven't looked in the bag?"

"Nope," I replied. "And Fleck wanted to. I told him no that it was your reward for being shot. Think of it as an apocalyptic secret Santa."

"Which, you know, works because Christmas is coming up."

"It is."

"What did you guys do last year?"

"Nothing really." When the words came out of my mouth, I felt sort of embarrassed. "Katie never asked, and the date kind of came and went."

"You mean Lev didn't want to celebrate it?"

"He did," I replied. "I said if Katie brought it up, we would. She never did. It was a hard one Sean."

"Yep, I know that. But I think we should bring it back for the kids. Speaking of bringing…I thought you'd bring June."

"Uh, yeah…" I shook my head. "No. They had cake and are now bouncing off the walls. I thought I'd save you that chaos. I did bring you cake though."

"So, Ben is with the sugar kids?"

"Yep."

Sean smiled, watching as I put his food on the tray. "Ben is like that character in an RV show or book that gets stuck with the kids because there's no storyline for him."

I laughed and handed Sean a fork. "That's funny, especially since he was bitching that they left him out of your surgery. Eat."

"Nila, I'm impressed. This looks really good. Spaghetti and chocolate cake. Did you make this?"

"You're cute. No, I am a horrible cook. Almada made this. It's very good." I sat down. "I kind of think this is all she knows how to make. Well, can make. She probably prefers Indian food but doesn't have the spices."

Sean looked at me.

"What?" I asked.

"Why would you say that?'

"She's Indian, that's no secret."

"That doesn't mean that's the only food she knows how to cook or even that she likes it."

"Ask Almada the next time you see her," I said.

"Ask me what?" Almada's voice entered the room. "How are you feeling, Sean?"

"Better, thank you," Sean replied, looking embarrassed.

"Doctor Peters said as long as you show no signs of infection, you can go to your place to recuperate. Lucky you, someone took care of that wound."

Sean must have thought she was joking, because he couldn't keep the sarcasm out of his voice when he said, "Yep. Bactine, duct tape, and a maxi pad. Best medical equipment in the field."

"I know, right?" Almada smiled. "Brilliant thinking on her part. Must be in the genes, her father is an incredible doctor."

I watched the expression on Sean's face, he wasn't amused.

"I'll let you eat," Almada said. "What was it, Nila, you wanted Sean to ask me?"

Sean shook his head. "She's being silly."

65

"No, I'm not," I replied. "He wants to know if Italian food is your specialty."

Almada chuckled. "Why? Because that's the only thing you've seen me cook. Your daughter loves it, and I couldn't get her to try anything I really cook well."

"Such as?" I asked.

"Nila," Sean spoke through clenched teeth.

"Indian food," she said. "Of course."

"Do you have all the spices you need?" I asked. "I mean, not sure what all they would be, but I know it takes some mixing them."

"It does," Almada answered. "And I have them, I managed to get them. I make a really great curry."

"I love curry," I said.

"Oh, then I will make you some. You can come over and we'll have a girls' night."

"Sounds like a plan."

Almada smiled again. "I'll let you two enjoy your visit. Sean, eat. I think Deacon McCaffrey is stopping in to see you."

"Swell," Sean said disgruntled.

"Oh, stop," I told him. "He's nice."

With a slight laugh, Almada backed up. "And on that disagreement, I'll let you two be. Good night."

I lifted my hand in a wave, then lifted the backpack once she left the room. "Before or after you eat?"

"During," Sean replied. "Open it up. I am dying to know what that deader had."

"Don't you think it's strange we find so much enjoyment in going through the belongings of a deader?"

"It tells their story. It makes them human," Sean said.

"That's a great way to look at it. Let's do this." I undid the zipper.

The more I looked at the red leather jacket, the angrier I got with that deader. There were things in there that made sense. Three cartons of cigarettes, two cans of spaghetti, Band-Aids, ibuprofen, a bottle of Canadian whiskey, and toilet paper, all crammed into that bag. But that jacket, that red leather jacket, was nothing less than a desecration of sacred ground.

"You can't be sure," Sean said.

"Oh, I'm positive," I replied. "That is Michael Jackson's jacket from the music video 'Thriller.' I know this because when Cade and I went to the museum, he was all sorts of fanboy info. How the *Night of the Living Dead* Museum in Monroeville had it and when they reopened the one in Evans City, they boasted about getting that back. Why would he do that Sean? Why?"

"You mean, take the jacket?"

"Yes."

"Because maybe he thought it would be useful in the up-coming winter."

"Please." I scoffed. "He wasn't fitting in it." I laid the coat flat on Sean's bed by his elevated leg. "I am really upset. We wanted to preserve that museum for generations to come."

"Let me see if I got this straight," he said. "You wanted to preserve a zombie apocalypse movie museum for future generations that survived a zombie apocalypse."

"Yes."

"Why would someone like Katie or June want to see that?" Sean asked.

"Because it is what we, as a people, envisioned it to be, and we got it all wrong. Look at this." I lifted the coat. "I'm gonna give this to Ben, he needs a warm coat."

"Ben?"

"Yes."

"Stop. He won't wear it."

"Yes, he will. Ben's also the only one thin enough to wear it." I turned when I heard the knock. When I looked, Finn McCaffrey was standing in the doorway.

"Can I come in?" he asked. "Oh, wow." He pointed as he walked in. "That coat is an amazing replica of the jacket Michael Jackson wore in the classic music video 'Thriller.'"

"*How?*" Sean questioned. "How do you even know that?"

"Big fan." Then Finn upped his voice and not only sang a couple lines from the song, unexpectedly, he did a few dance steps. "Thriller."

I clapped.

Sean did not.

Finn produced a half-crooked smile, drummed up a bashful look and tossed out his hand. "Hate to say it, but I'm not here for entertainment."

Sean blurted out a, "Thank God."

I, of course, let out an "aw," which prompted a side-eyed look from Sean.

I didn't defend my dismay, and it really was disappointing, albeit briefly.

That moment, with the imitation Michal Jackson singing and the little four seconds of memorized dance moves caused a genuine feeling of happiness I hadn't felt in a long time. A smile that was real, not forced.

It was just something spontaneous and funny that seemed to get lost in our world.

"What's up?" asked Sean.

"First, how are you feeling?" Finn asked.

"Sore, but better," Sean replied.

"I heard her aim was really bad."

"To say the least."

"I guess her medical skills are better than her defensive skills."

"Seriously?" Sean asked.

"Yeah." Finn nodded. "She's going to get recognized by council for measures taken to save your life."

"She shot me."

"Minor detail in the light of the fact that she saved your life."

Again, Finn caused me to smile, no, wait, laugh. Although I don't think he meant it.

Both men glanced at me as if I were mad.

"Why is that funny?" Finn asked.

"Marsha is nice. Very Minnesota," I said, then began a rant. "However, she wouldn't have to take any lifesaving measures if she hadn't shot for a deader in the first place. Rule number one: no noise unless absolutely necessary. And...and...she used a freaking maxi pad, super absorbent maxi pad, duct tape, and expired Bactine. Plus, Sean was nowhere near needing lifesaving measures. It was a cheap, old, twenty-two with a slightly bent barrel that limited the aim, not to mention the fire power. Deadly wound, that's hysterical because the shell was sticking partially out like a white head pimple and if Sean wasn't being such a dick, I would have pulled it out in the store."

I exhaled.

"Done?" Finn asked.

"I think so, yes." I nodded.

Sean looked at me. "You really could have pulled it out?"

"Yeah, you didn't need surgery, please." I waved out my hand. "A topical numbing agent, like a freezing spray, sterile water and big toenail tweezer, a good squeeze, pull and scream from you…" I snapped my finger. "Right out."

"Like you've done it before?" Sean asked.

"Oh, yeah. Did it for Darren Lowenstein in the back of Lev's Chevy so we wouldn't get in trouble when Bobby shot Darren in the ass."

"I'm curious," Finn said. "Did anyone ever find out?"

"Yep. Lev told," I replied. "He was such a tattle tale."

Sean huffed. "If you could have taken it out, why didn't you?"

Before I could answer, Finn did. "She said you were being a dick. Didn't you hear that part?" He then glanced at me. "You know, Nila, I know you have done a fantastic job of keeping your group together and protected. Your attitude is amazing. I really think you should serve in some leadership capacity in the Colonies. You have great leadership quali-ties."

"I was team lead at Arby's.

"I loved Arby's," Finn said. "Anyhow, think about it. I wish I could use you now, but with the babies, that's too risky."

"What's going on?" I asked.

"The reason I came," Finn said. "Sean, as soon as you are physically ready, I need you to return to duty. I'm willing to look past your AWOL stint. I need you. Either here on patrol or in the field."

"I'll repeat her question," said Sean. "What's going on?"

"Evans City was clear," Finn replied. "We had just been there two days earlier. So, it's easy to say a hoard moved in, attacked those campers or whatever and moved on. But we have a man that studies the movement of what you call the deaders. They don't migrate like that. They kind of stay in one area that catches their attention. Ragers, well, they move on instinct and sight, but if they don't see anyone, they just try to make it home. Make sense?"

I nodded.

"We think those three recently turned you encountered were part of a group that uses the deaders as a weapon."

"A weapon to what?" I asked. "Deaders don't spread the virus. The virus needs a live host. Ragers do until they die."

Sean interjected. "I don't think he means as a weapon to infect people, I think he means as a weapon to scavenge camps and towns."

"Exactly," said Finn. "Lead in the dead, take what they can, move on. We have been seeing this pattern for a while. In this case, they knew Evans City was already a dead or clear area, so they led in a small group just in case, while they cleaned out the town. But they got sick and there went that."

"What makes you think those three ragers were part of this group, if there is one?" I asked. "I mean it sounds pretty farfetched."

"Does it?" Finn asked. "We think this because we went into the town before sundown, that was what eight hours after you guys returned here?" He shrugged. "All that remained were the ones you killed and the ragers, which were easy to spot. The rest gone and deaders don't move on like that."

Sean exhaled. "Unless they're led. How stupid can people be? Really. We're trying to get rid of them, not breed more."

I corrected his statement. "They aren't breeding more they're just killing people. The deaders don't spread it. They never did. My brother, Bobby, was working on this virus nearly a year before it got out of control. People got infected then turned, in that stage of infection before death they spread it more. Then you know, it freaking mutated to an avian strain. H2Z1 they should call it."

Finn chuckled. "That's good. My point is, Evans City is close. If they were there, which I believe they were, they're gonna find the Colonies, this one especially in this area and a few small towns that we found still surviving between here and Ohio."

"What are we worried about?" I asked. "There were a few dozen dead. A few good shooters at the perimeters can take them down."

Sean shook his head. "They only used a few dozen in a dead town. How many would they send in here?"

I scoffed a laugh. "Like how many could they have?"

Finn answered, "Thousands. They're gathering them. Leading them. They bring a thousand to us, we're done."

"How do you know they have thousands?" I asked.

"There's a section of I-80 blocked off with trucks, sealing thousands—they're like sardines," Finn replied. "And that's just one group. There could be more, they could be networking. You may think it's farfetched, but anything is possible."

Sean asked, "We know for a fact about the highway deaders?"

Finn nodded. "We had a team see them, there were too many to take out with what they had. They also didn't spot any of the group that led them, but there was a camp set up nearby in an RV parking lot."

"Oh my God," I gasped. "Fleck and I ran into a scenario like that. No deaders, but it looked like a camp surrounded by trucks, but there was also a camp on the outside. If it was the same group, they moved west."

"Or staying in the area," Finn said. "Either way we have to protect this place, and we need to send people out there to look for these hoards and the groups that are leading them. I don't have the manpower to do both. If I send people out, I need people to take over on the fences and vulnerable areas. I also need to put together an evacuation team."

I nodded. "That's why you're keeping everyone in the schools. Count me in to walk a perimeter or sit in a sniper's position. I may be pregnant, but I can do that."

Sean pointed at me. "You'll want her. She's the best shot I've seen. Count me in as well."

"Thank you," Finn said. "Do you think Phil Fleckenstien would be interested?'

That made me laugh. "Fleck, we call him Fleck," I said. "And yeah, he'll help. Ask him, I'm sure he'll say yes. He's not the best shot, but he's good with the deaders."

"I'll do that. Thank you. Sean." Finn extended his hand and shook Sean's. "Get well, thank you again." He turned to me. "And find me tomorrow and we'll get you a post."

"Will do."

Finn walked to the door. "If you think of anyone else…"

"You can ask Miss Minnesota," I suggested. "If she's aiming at a hoard, she'll hit something."

"Yeah, I think we need to conserve ammo. I'll put her in the clinic since she does a mad field dressing." He joked, winked and walked out.

Sean shook his head after Finn left.

"What?" I asked.

"He's really not that funny."

"Stop. He's nice and…I'm glad you're gonna do this."

"I want to do this." He looked at me. "Knowing there's a threat out there. And June, the kids, you in here. What choice do we have? We need to keep everyone safe. What I'd like to do is go out with a demolition team and wipe out that hoard."

"Do it."

"I have June."

"Ben and I can watch June; you won't be gone long. And knowing that you're out there taking care of things," I said, "will make me feel a whole lot better in here."

FOURTEEN

ADAPTING

Sean

December 12

Eight miles east of Cleveland, I worried we were going to be stranded when the unexpected snow started to fall fast all around us.

The trucks were big enough to handle the untreated roads, but not at the rate the snow was falling.

One of the guys on my crew assured me that because it was a lake effect snowfall, it probably was localized to where we were investigating.

It had been six weeks since Finn McCaffrey came into my hospital room and informed Nila and me about the marauders that were using deaders as weapons. Admittedly, I didn't believe it at first. To me it was stupid. Who would put their own lives at risk like that? Surely there were other ways to plunder and pillage camps and towns?

I was only out of commission for ten days, and then I went with Steve and Carla, two soldiers from The Colony, to investigate the wrangled hoard on I-80.

A previous scouting party said they were gone and were trying to locate them.

If there was a group of deaders a thousand strong, surely they'd be easy to spot.

And they were.

Soon, I saw with my own eyes the tractor trailer pen that kept them in. It didn't look like they had broken free, one truck had to be moved to release them.

Carla was a former detective with the Capitol Police and put that hat back on when she was at the scene. A camp was set up nearby. She figured the group had at least twenty people and two big trucks.

It seemed fictional.

That was my first trip.

I made a couple trips out there, usually every ten days, with my team to look for large groups of deaders in our area, and the marauder group, of course. Nothing was near us and that was a good thing.

There were never more than three or four of us, not enough to take out any hoard or engage in a battle with a group. We were scouts.

There were other teams created to 'engage.'

My team was considered investigative scouts. We looked, we reported, and we went home.

This trip though, I knew we shouldn't have left. Winter in the north was always unpredictable, but I also knew it was close to Christmas and I wanted to see what I could get on our road trip.

"Yeah, I don't know about this," I said as Steve pulled the truck onto the snow-covered road.

"I am telling you, in three miles, there'll be zero snow," Steve replied.

"Lake effect." Carla read through her notes. "You'll see. And I really want to hit that Walmart we saw in Wadsworth. It looked untouched."

Steve nodded. "Sounds like a plan. Let's just be happy we're not the team driving to get Almada. That part of the country gets slammed by the coast."

He had a point. Almada had left two weeks earlier to go to a lab in Maryland that they had been preparing for her. Somehow, I knew it had to do with the second amniocentesis they did on Nila. Almada had mentioned something about a DNA marker in the second baby, the one that was infected.

She had to try something. She had hit a wall with the cure.

"To be honest," Carla said from the backseat. "I don't see the point."

"In a cure?" I asked. "Are you nuts, the virus is still out there."

"Is it?" she asked. "Weather is getting cold; dead are slowing down. We had three people with it."

Steve shook his head. "In our Colony. It's out there. But I see what you're saying. My reasoning is, why are they bothering? What they get for the cure is what they make from the weird girl.

"Katie," I corrected. "And okay, she's a bit strange."

"But they stopped," Steve said. "McCaffrey said to give her a break. They can't mass produce it? And the doses are like gold."

"Maybe that's why she went to Maryland," I said. "Maybe there's a way at that lab to reproduce it."

Steve shrugged. "I think they should try out west."

I laughed. "What's out west? The same as here."

"No, man, have you been out there?"

"No, have you?"

"No, but I met a dude who says Washington State is fine. He said parts of Oregon, Vancouver, and Alaska. Untouched."

Almost mumbling from her face buried in a file, Carla said, "And where did you meet this...dude?"

"When I was in the Minnesota Colony."

"Yep. If it was so fine out there, why did he leave?" she asked.

"Looking for his family," Steve replied. "I'm telling you. It's not everywhere. Look how long Ontario held out. I mean we're all running around calling it the apocalypse."

"It is," I said.

"Hear me out," stated Steve. "What if it's not? What if there are places out west and north and other parts of the world that are unaffected?"

"If that's true," I said. "Why aren't they helping us?"

"Too little. Too late. Maybe they're just waiting for us all to die out."

"While your theory is good," I said, shaking my head. "I refuse to believe that out there, somewhere, civilization is fine and we're just dying off."

"You believe that, and I'll believe out there is a better world," Steve said.

"Why don't you go?" I asked.

"For the same reason you refuse to believe it. I am not gonna cut bait and run. I'm fighting," Steve said then let out a huge, "ha!"

I jumped a little. "What?"

"And with six miles. The snow is nonexistent."

Peering out the windshield, it didn't look like a single flake had fallen. Steve was right. It would be nice if he was right about things being normal out west and farther north, but the realist in me knew he couldn't be. Unlike the lake effect snow, the possibility of a deader apocalypse just disappearing at the crossing of miles, just wasn't a reality.

FIFTEEN

ALTERING

Fleck

It became our routine on the nights Nila took rooftop watch, and I'd go over to have dinner with them. Usually, Ben or Marsha would cook. Never Nila, thank God, and I'd take Katie after we ate to play with her dog.

I loved that we did it, I liked the feel of family; I acted like it annoyed me, but it didn't. I wasn't sure what I would do if I didn't have the cabin gang.

We sat around the table, like the world was normal.

June was finally trying to sit in a real chair instead of that booster I tripped over all the time.

Ben likes to joke that I should have never moved out, to which I told him, it was the same thing as being a grandparent. A grandparent could give the kid back when they were done, and I could just go home.

Unless you were Ben, who raised Sawyer.

At least no one yelled at me for being on the toilet too long.

"Fleck, do you want to see my book when we get back?" Katie asked. "I can read it to you."

"Are you still working on the story about the family?"

"It takes time. I'm almost done."

"Yeah. I'm always up for critiquing you."

"Oh Fleckie," Marsha gave me a playful tap. "Be nice."

"Katie?" Nila asked as she turned from the table. "How come you haven't shown me the book?"

"You'll know the story when it's done, Mommy. I need to show Fleck. He sees things in the drawings."

"Picture books are my forte," I joked. "I bet you have a great ending planned. I mean you gotta have like twenty drawings in it."

Katie nodded. "I hope the ending works out. It would be sad if it didn't. I don't know what I am going to do or how. I have to figure it out. I'm gonna have to be the hero. I don't want to but I am."

Marsha spoke up, "You betcha everyone loves a reluctant hero. It's gonna be buttons to the wall good."

Katie giggled.

I thought it was funny too. Marsha always had these crazy sayings that didn't make sense.

"Oh!" Marsha blurted out startling us all. "I have to go. I have clinic duty." She stood.

"I'll walk with you," Nila said. "Ben are you good with all the kids till Sean gets back?"

"I'm fine. I don't work the clinic until tomorrow afternoon," Ben replied. "Be careful. And Marsha, I've been hearing good things about you down there."

"Gosh, that means a lot. I'm still learning."

She darted a kiss to my cheek. Marsha was doing well and had come a long way in eight weeks since the maxi pads and duct tape. While I thought it was brilliant, her father was appalled for some reason and put her on a crash course to medicine.

Nila tried to do the same with Marsha with her shooting but that never got better, at least from what I could see. The last time I took her hunting, she aimed for a buck and hit a tree ten feet away to her right.

Katie put on her shoes and her obnoxiously bright pink coat Sean had picked up on his last run.

It was bulky and had this fur hood that buried her little face.

"It's not that cold, Katie," I told her.

"We'll be outside. I like my coat. Don't you?"

"No, you can see you a mile away."

Another Katie giggle, and she ran to the door. "Good."

I shook my head and followed her out.

We were outside a very short time, especially when we went in the evening. Usually, Katie was running the whole time chasing her dog, making off the wall comments.

Lately, she had been driving Max, the handler, a little nuts. He had been snippy to her about her instructions regarding Caesar, and I had to tell him about it.

"Max doesn't like you," Katie said as we arrived. "So be nice."

"Oh, he can deal. Tough titty on him."

Katie stopped and looked at me. "Tough titty. What does that mean?"

"Don't worry about it and don't tell your mother I said that."

"I will."

"Of course, you will."

"Let's go get the dogs."

Katie ran ahead of me and then just stopped cold. Fifteen feet ahead, in the middle of the dog room, she didn't move, it was as if she were in some sort of frozen state.

I waited.

Did she see something?

Was she having a seizure? I never knew her to be so still when she wasn't sleeping.

"Katie. Hey." I snapped my finger a couple times. "Are you okay?"

Slowly, she turned around with a really puzzled look on her face. Then the puzzled look turned into some sort of 'Oh wow, I got it' look as she walked back to me.

I prepared myself for her to bring up the tough titty comment or maybe she finally figured out the ending of that book.

"Fleck?'

"Yes, Katie." I waited for it.

"Did you know Lev had a son?"

The words stammered in shock as they came from my mouth. "Wait? W… what? Katie, where in the world is this coming from?"

She shrugged. "Did you know?"

"That Lev had a son?" I shook my head. "No, I didn't."

"Hmm. Neither did he."

And on that she darted off as if she didn't just say the oddest, out of the blue thing again.

I made a mental note to bring it up to Nila, it was just the strangest thing to say.

Mostly, I had stopped being shocked by what came out of Katie's mouth, but this time she got me.

SIXTEEN

EMBEDDED HOPE

Nila

December 13

Ration day. It was a cute little set up where we went into the
school kitchen and picked our allotted amounts for the week.
The only thing that wasn't there was fresh meat. The canning
committee had canned some, but I liked when we hunted.
That wasn't exactly easy for me anymore though, in fact it
was even getting harder for me to just move around, let alone
hunt. My growing belly was exploding, and I still had sixteen
weeks to go.

I was managing.

Except bladder control. No one prepared me for that
while carrying twins. Especially when I laughed hard, and I
had been laughing about Fleck since the night before.

With such urgency he sought me out on my watch to tell
me what Katie had said about Lev having a son he didn't
know about.

For a split second, I was like, 'Oh my God, who would
do such a horrible thing to Lev and not tell him he had a
child?', then it hit me, and I laughed.

"Of course, Lev has a son he doesn't know about," I told
Fleck. "One of the boys in my belly."

"Are you sure she meant that? She has these psychic thoughts."

"Positive. I'm not doubting that it hit her like a premonition or intuition thing," I told him. "But Katie isn't old enough to realize that Lev is the father and how that came about."

It wasn't the wayward suggestion of my daughter, it was Fleck's reaction to it that made me laugh. No matter how many times I told him Katie meant the babies I was carrying, he insisted she didn't.

I even laughed out loud while trying to pick out my canned vegetable.

"What's so funny?" I heard Sean ask.

I turned around. "Hey, is it your ration day, too?"

"It is. I thought you knew that."

"I probably did." I noticed him taking a closer look at the vegetables. "Do you see something interesting?'

"No, I'm trying to see why you were laughing."

"Oh." I waved out my hand and grabbed the beans. "Katie made one of her off the wall, out of the blue comments to Fleck and he was freaking out."

"Was he dying again?"

"No." I shook my head. "She told him that Lev had a son he didn't know about."

"Of course, the twins."

"Thank you. Exactly. But he is convinced out there in the world is a mini Lev."

"There will be," Sean said. "Wow, it must be everyone's ration day."

I crinkled my brow, curious as to what he meant and saw Almada. "She doesn't look like she's getting rations, she's coming this way."

"She looks tired," commented Sean.

"Yeah, she does.'

Despite how tired she looked, Almada smiled. "Glad I found you."

"Is something wrong?"

Almada shook her head. "No, might be hopeful. Can you meet me in my office when you're done?"

"Sure. Absolutely."

"Thanks." And then she walked away.

"I wonder what she wants," I said.

"Probably has to do with her testing," Sean suggested. "Remember I mentioned that she said something about Baby A having some sort of markers?"

"Yeah, but I didn't understand that. Did you want to come?"

"Do you mind?"

"Not at all."

For some reason what Sean said suddenly made sense. She had left Alpha Colony to go to Maryland right after my second amniocentesis.

We finished up our ration grab and headed to her office before taking the items home.

Almada was seated behind her desk looking pretty serious. For a second, I worried, but she had said nothing was wrong.

Sean and I both sat down across from her like some couple preparing for a medical diagnosis.

"So," Almada said, folding her hands. "As you probably guessed, my main reason for going to Maryland was to see if we could create a cure or vaccine in mass quantities. The lab has the ability to create doses, but it would take a year or so to get everyone we need vaccinated. By then I believe or rather believed, the virus would go into herd immunity."

"You're saying in a year we won't have to worry?" I asked.

"That's what I thought, then I was quickly shot down. It's here to stay, like the flu, like the common cold. Here. Forever."

"What about the rumor about Alaska?" I asked. "Have you heard it?'

I quickly looked at Sean. "What rumor?"

Almada answered. "That Washington State, Vancouver and Alaska are deader free."

"I heard that one before. Remember Ontario?" I said. "Lev almost died there because they were doing everything in their power to stop it. No matter how extreme."

Almada nodded. "They didn't have a cure. I think things would have been different if they did. As far as what is out west, we're just hearing about this, and Finn is looking into it. If it is true, we'll move all the colonies that way. But if it's true, we better come knocking with a cure."

"Why did you ask to talk to me?" I questioned.

"As you know we had to slow down on Katie. It was a lot on her, before I get into explaining why I asked you here, I want to give you some background science."

I lifted my hand. "Please keep it layman. I get lost on that stuff."

Almada nodded. "Absolutely. In 2010 scientists were able to successfully create a self-replicating synthetic bacterial cell. Then they moved on to viruses, good ones, because it was believed that some viruses could attack cancer cells and wipe them out. In 2021, they perfected the self-replicating synthetic cell. For example, they could take a cell from a human, replicate it and that in turn would replicate. As you know it take decades for a procedure to get approval and the world ended."

"What does this have to do with my babies? I asked.

"I'm getting there," Almada stated. "Let's jump ahead to our virus. One of the biggest reasons we were never able to stop it was because it was such an original strain, we needed patient zero or zeroes, because we believe there were several that were infected at the same time. We never found where they started. Katie's immunity shows that at some point, she was exposed to a variation of the virus and her body beat it."

Sean interjected. "I believe she was bit by her father."

I nodded. "She was."

"That was probably it. Anyhow, Katie's cells produced an antibody cure. The problem is, it's not permanent. We need something that will cure it and prevent it. Much like catching Chicken Pox."

"How do you do something like that?" I asked.

"When someone is infected, we do gene therapy," Almada replied.

I shook my head. "You guys took bone marrow from me and—"

Almada cut me off. "Totally different. Gene therapy uses the patient's own cells to cure, replicate, however you want to say it. Instead of doing that, we take a synthetic replicating cell and use that. A cell that is genetically immune to the virus. Once a person is given that therapy, they will never have to worry about a bite or the virus again."

Sean asked. "Katie's can't do that?"

Almada shook her head. "We can't do a synthetic cell based on Katie's. I mean we can, but it's a one-shot deal, and using gene therapy for a one-shot deal, it's easy to just treat like we did with Ben and Fleck."

"Baby A," I whispered in revelation. "He has that. That's why I'm here."

"He does." Almada nodded. "I am not sure how or why, but he exhibits the closest we believe it can get to the patient zero strain. Maybe it was because Lev was infected when you conceived."

"So, you just need his cells?" I asked.

"Yes. But therein lies a problem," Almada explained. "He's infected. One hundred percent has the virus."

"But he's still alive," I said.

"Yes. Sadly, he is going to be in a perpetual state of what you call a rager until he is cured. We have one day at max to do that. Then, and this is all theory, we do gene therapy to keep his cells healthy enough. The answer is in his DNA, but to get good cells to replicate, we do gene therapy with a close match, like we would do with a bone marrow transplant."

"Katie or Baby B?" I asked.

"Yes," Almada answered. "The doctors and scientists I worked with in Maryland believe this is it. This is the end of the virus killing our world. And it starts with curing your baby and hoping Katie or Baby B are a match. If they are ..."

My emotional gasp cut her off. I don't think they under-stood what slammed into me at that moment. Maybe Almada thought I was angry or shocked or I didn't want to do it.

That wasn't the case at all.

I gasped with emotions, my heart suddenly felt full, and it took me a second to breathe and stop myself from crying.

"What is it?" Sean asked.

"Lev. This means, if this works," I said, my voice cracking with each word. "Lev's death wasn't in vain."

Maybe they didn't understand, but I did. His catching the virus wasn't for nothing. Lev was not going to be a statistic in this screwed up world, another memory or person we lost.

Lev would never know it, but I would. He found a way to live on and be a hero in all of this.

It was more of a healing moment, than anyone would ever know.

It renewed me with hope and in my mind, there was no way things were going to go bad again.

PART TWO

FROM HOME

SEVENTEEN

EMPTY PROMISES

Nila

January 12

I was still reveling in the happiness that celebrating Christmas once again brought to me. It was stress-free and while I did have times of sadness over Addy, Paul and Lev, the joy on my daughter's face when she woke to find her gifts said so much. But it was more than the gifts, it was the time together. All of us talked about favorite holidays, relaxing, and laughing about old times.

A dead world didn't enter our day, and hope was on the horizon.

In the four weeks since Almada told me about Baby Lev, she updated me often.

They were making great progress in Maryland. It was a matter of waiting until the baby was born and cured.

I believed he would be cured. I was so positive I started calling him by his name, Lev.

Earl was Baby B.

I know Fleck joked about naming the infected twin after Lev, but I needed to. It was fitting.

My child would be the answer to ending all the madness, at least getting it to a point where it wasn't a concern.

I needed it to be a 'Lev' that did that.

Katie's voice woke me along with some bleeps and buzzes. I wasn't sure what she was saying or what the noise was, they came from the other room. I was cozy and warm in my bed, and knew right away by the chill in the air, that the temperature outside had dropped.

The building wasn't the warmest and everyone was on conservation.

I decided to get out of bed, do a quick clean up and go get my half cup of allotted morning coffee.

My back hurt, my legs ached, the pregnancy still a long way from being over, was truly taking its toll. I had twelve weeks to go but, in reality, it probably was eight.

Marsha said her father planned on coming back to the colony six weeks before my due date.

Hopefully, the weather would be good.

It wasn't looking that way this morning.

It seemed like such a great morning; I should have known.

Ben was at the kitchen table with Katie who was working on something. Sawyer was in the living room playing a video game from the eighties that Sean had found at some antique shop. I sipped my coffee and looked out the window. The snow started to fall. We were spared any real snow, which was unusual for western Pennsylvania.

"Hoping it will snow or not?" Ben asked.

I turned from the window. "Either. I don't care." I noticed he lifted his mug of coffee that he read an actual newspaper. "What year is that from?"

"Titanic." He flipped to show me the front cover. "Sean found some treasures."

"He did. Although I got a compass watch." I lifted my arm showing the big bulky thing.

"You never know when you'll need one."

"Yeah." I laughed and sat down, noticing Katie was actually writing instead of drawing. "What are you doing?" I asked.

"Planning,"

"Planning what?"

She glanced up to me. "Sometimes it helps to write down what you're going to do."

"That's true."

"I'm going to take Caesar, Mommy, is that okay?"

"Take Caesar?" I asked.

"On a big adventure."

"Oh, that sounds fun," I said.

"It's very serious."

I smiled at my daughter imagining Fleck's dismay at whatever she would have him doing at the dog visit.

"When will this be?" I asked.

Katie shrugged. "I'm not sure. Definitely before the baby is born."

"Babies," I corrected.

There was a knock at the door, startling me and taking my attention away from Katie. I looked down at my extra-large watch. It was early.

"Want me to get it?" asked Ben.

"No, read your 1912 paper." Holding my coffee, I stood and walked to the door. To my surprise it was Finn, Marsha and little June.

I couldn't help it, my smile and greeting were awkward.

"What's going on?" I asked.

"Hiya, Nila," Marsha giggled. "I love how that rhymes."

"It really doesn't, anyhow, what's up?" I asked again.

"Was wondering if I can steal you and Ben," Finn stated. "I need to talk to you both."

"What about Fleck?" I questioned.

"We're going to where he is. Sean's on his way."

Marsha spoke up. "That's why I have this one." She referred to June.

"Um, yeah, sure." I opened the door wider. "Come in. I'll get dressed."

Ben stood from the table as they entered. "Wow, sounds like a secret meeting," he said jokingly. "Must be important."

"More than you realize," Finn replied. "It is."

When Finn said he needed to talk to us, I had no idea it meant getting in the truck, and driving a few blocks on the slick road to the deconstruction area. No one lived there and it was fenced off for the most part. Some spots by the wooded area didn't look too secure, almost nonexistent. Nature provided protection, that was the section bordered by a creek that led to a mountainous area.

I suppose there wasn't too much of a worry about it; deaders had a hard time even without the cold moving on uneven land. That was why we had very few wandering dead at the cabin.

There were several work trucks parked about and it was noisy with hammers and saws, men yelling back and forth.

Fleck worked there. He was part of a crew, each assigned to a house. They were stripping the insides for wood, viable furniture, anything that could be used again.

Six deaders had gathered. They held on to the chain link fence, moving in slow motion, the cold slowed them down so much.

The moment I saw them I had a feeling maybe he wanted to speak to us about the marauders who used deaders as an invasion weapon.

Surely, they had to go south because if they knew deaders, their weapon was useless when temperatures were below thirty degrees.

Sean was outside a yellow house when we arrived, waiting for us, I guess.

Ben looked around. "This seems very strange to gather us," he said. "Why?"

"All of you are a family," Finn replied. "Let's go inside."

I got out of the truck first and my feet sloshed in the wet snow. I walked up to Sean, whispering, "Do you know why we're meeting?"

He shook his head. "No. Fleck's waiting inside. Let's get in. It's cold."

"Why didn't you go in?" I asked.

"Come on, hang out with Fleck? No." Sean opened the door for me.

It was warm inside, the small living room was heated by a kerosene heater. Five chairs were there in a circle.

"Fleck?" I asked. "Do you know what's going on?"

"He said he wanted to talk."

"Super-secret," I said, taking a seat. "Is The Colony bugged?"

Finn replied as he walked in, "No. But you never know who is listening. Out here no one is. Please, everyone sit down."

"You know," Fleck said. "You dragged everyone out here. Someone had to see you. What's your story?'

"That I want opinions on if this area needs to be shut down and swept." Finn waved out his hand. "We won't be out here that long." Finn sat. "How many more weeks do you have Nila?"

"Twelve," I answered.

"Ben, as a doctor, what is the concern when it comes to premature delivery?"

"For the babies?" Ben asked. "The lungs are the main issue. Usually around thirty-two weeks gestation we worry less about that. What's going on?"

"All of you." Finn leaned forward folding his hands. "All of you operate as one big family, and as a family you don't keep secrets. I would be surprised if what I am about to say is news to any of you." He looked around. "You know and have been told to keep it secret that Baby A, or Baby Lev, carries a unique genetic marker that means once he has been cured, he has the ability to provide the genetics to create the perfect artificial cell that will end all this madness."

It was quiet in our circle for a few seconds.

Then Fleck exhaled and sat back. "Well, so much for not letting anyone know."

"We knew it would get out," I said. "Almada couldn't keep her work in Maryland secret for too long. We knew that."

"I'm confused," Sean said. "Why the secret meeting? Since you know, we all know."

"Because I know more," Finn replied. "Nila, you will have the babies. They will use Baby B to cure baby Lev. If that works—"

"They start working on the artificial gene," I cut him off.

"Yes and no. They work on it. They cure the baby," Finn said. "But they're going to tell you he died. More than likely right after he is delivered. They'll take him away and claim he had breathing problems, and then they'll tell you he died."

Every single bit of air escaped my body at that second. Fleck's, Sean's and Ben's voices of surprise were muffled beneath the blood that immediately flowed to my ears.

"What?" I asked, shocked.

Finn repeated, "They will cure him, but more than likely they think you won't know that because you'll think that he died. They'll ask for his body so they could try to do the cure anyhow. The truth is they need him one hundred percent to use."

Ben lifted his hand. "Wait. Weren't they going to anyhow? I mean, why say he died?"

Sean groaned out, "So, they could have the body. The body, Ben. They don't care if he lives or dies, they need what is in him."

My hand shot to my mouth.

Fleck asked, "How long have you known?'

"About two weeks." Finn lifted his hand. "And I have been working on a plan ever since, that's why I didn't say anything sooner."

"Screw that." Fleck threw out his hand. "We pack up and we leave."

"You can't do that!" Sean argued. "Baby Lev is infected, he needs to be cured, they can do that here. If he is born without a cure, he will die. And then what? Go where? Back to the cabin? They'll find us. You wanna run with Nila pregnant in this weather? Deaders or not. It's not an option."

"Staying is not an option," Fleck barked. "We have to leave."

"Again," Sean replied. "And go where?"

Finn spoke up, "Alaska."

It drew an immediate silence.

Finn nodded. "Those rumors are true. There are six areas in this world operating as its own country, its own entity, infection free. I planned on going there, me and a couple of my men, and have been setting things up. Colonies are also supposedly hand-picking people to go. This new development escalates that plan. In four weeks, ships will make a weekly trip for about a month, they'll be selective. You either have one hell of a talent or be part of an accepted group, like from the colonies. After that, the border is shut down."

"How do you know this?" Sean asked.

"Communication channels are open; you guys just don't have the access that I do."

Ben asked, "You want us to go to Alaska? Before or after the babies are born?"

"After," Finn replied. "You need the cure."

"What if," I spoke up, "we take Almada with us, she can cure the baby after he's born. We won't need to stay here. I mean if she knew of this plan, she would be livid, she—" I stopped talking when I saw the drawn look on Finn's face. "She knows, doesn't she?"

"Yes." Finn nodded once. "Rosen said it was her idea."

I gasped.

Fleck freaked out. "I'm killing her. I knew it. I knew it from the second she gassed us."

Finn pointed. "You won't say anything. Nothing. Who is to say she won't take Nila again, or Katie? Just let things play out."

I asked, "Doctor Rosen? So, he knows? He must do if he told you it was Almada's idea."

"He knows, but he will be the reason we can pull this off," Finn said. "You need to have the babies, allow them to cure Baby Lev, let them tell you he died, and then all of you leave. Take off. I will have a safe passage for you to an area outside of Colony Three in Nashville. I will meet you with the baby. From there we head to Texas where there'll be a flight to take us to Seattle and I can get us on a ship."

Fleck scoffed. "This is all too clean and planned out."

"I've had a couple weeks to tweak it."

"And they're just gonna hand you the baby?"

"Yes." Finn nodded. "Doctor Rosen will declare the baby deceased, and he will prepare the baby for me to take. We've spoken."

Again, Fleck was skeptical. "And they're gonna just hand him over to you? How do you know?"

"How do you think I found out?" Finn retorted. "I am in charge of escorting the transport of the baby to the lab. Because of my position in the colonies, I am overseeing it. They won't think anything of it."

Sean said, "Until you go south when you're supposed to go east."

Finn shook his head. "Who is going to tell? My team? They're going to Alaska. By the time they realize I didn't make it to Maryland or Alaska, we will be on our way to that plane in Texas. Trust me, this is the only way. If you don't do this," he looked at me. "You won't see the baby."

I immediately stood up, my heart racing, my hand to my mouth. It was unbelievable what I was hearing, it didn't seem true.

Ben grabbed my hand. "Nila, are you okay?"

I shook my head. "No. Ben, Baby Lev is the key to ending this. Curing it for everyone. How can I take that cure and run to Alaska?"

"You can't be serious?" Ben asked, standing. "This is your child, Nila. To hell with the needs of the many, this is your child. They will test him, use him, all for the purpose of science. He will not live. There is no choice, we have to run."

"I know, but can I do so and say screw the cure, screw the world? If we go to Alaska, what's to say an outbreak won't happen there and we're back to square one?"

Sean tossed out his hands. "Then we're back to square one, with a living breathing baby to live on."

"Nila," Fleck said. "I know this is all a lot. It's a lot to take in for all of us. But if you're confused, it's Lev's child. Ask yourself, 'What would Lev say?'"

What would Lev say?

Now there was a sentence no one had said to me for a while.

What would Lev say? I didn't have to ponder that for very long, I saw him in my head, felt Lev in my heart, and heard him in my ears.

Finn also stood and faced me. "Think about it."

I shook my head. "I don't need to. This is Lev's child," I said. "And I know what Lev would say."

EIGHTEEN

EMPTY THOUGHTS

Sean

Nila had a look on her face that showed her inner turmoil. I got it, I did. I just didn't understand where her sudden love for the entire human race came from. For the first time, Fleck and I were in agreement. Only he was more outspoken, and slightly outraged, when we returned to my apartment after the meeting with Finn.

Before relieving Marsha from kid duty, we needed another meeting. The four of us.

"Why is this such a problem for you, right now?" Fleck asked Nila. "I mean, you look genuinely torn."

"I am," she replied.

"Why?" barked Fleck. "Seriously why? This is the same woman who poisoned the well without batting an eye."

"Oh my God," Nila gasped. "Why are you bringing that up?"

"Because it's true. And for the first time I know what Lev would say. Lev would say," Fleck then went on to do his Lev imitation. "Nila poisoned the well, why do you suddenly care? We need to worry about us. So," Fleck returned to normal. "Get your shit together Nila."

"What is the solution?" Nila asked.

"You have the babies," Fleck answered. "And in the meantime, we get ready to roll. When they are born, we don't let either of them out of our sight and we go."

"Go where?" I asked.

"If Alaska is real, then that's where we go. Ships are picking people up, right?" Fleck asked. "We bleed pretty boy Finn for information, and we go ourselves."

Nila shook her head. "It doesn't make sense. Why would Almada want to kill my baby?"

"I think she wants the baby in the name of science," I answered.

"But it's my child."

Fleck scoffed. "She doesn't have any. She doesn't care. She probably is thinking that hey, you're having two, you won't mind if one dies."

I cringed. "Fleck, stop, okay. Not cool." I turned to Ben. "You've been quiet. What are your thoughts?"

Ben took a few seconds to think about his answer. "I don't know. I mean, if we believe what Finn is telling us about the baby, then why don't we trust him enough to get us to Alaska? If there is mistrust in Finn, then why are we believing what he is saying about Almada?"

"Like maybe it's Finn that wants the baby?" I asked. "Remember I told you guys she was suspicious about Finn and the people on council."

Ben shrugged. "Could be. I'm not saying he is. But what if that's the case. Maybe Almada doesn't want the baby to die, and Finn planned to take him to Maryland all along. He gets us to Nashville out of the way."

Nila paced some. "I don't know. I do know that I don't want to go to Alaska. I don't. I want to go home to the cabin."

Ben approached her. "And if they want the baby that badly, that is the first place they'll look. They hit us once, they'll get us again."

"Okay," Fleck said. "Let's stop. Other than the fact that we can't stay here. What all can we agree on?" He lifted his hand. "Baby Lev is prime real estate."

"He needs to be cured," Ben stated.

"We can't stay here," I said.

Fleck looked at me. "I said other than the fact we can't stay here."

"Sorry. We can't do the cabin."

"We don't know if Alaska is really an option," Nila said. "So, we're back to square one. We don't have a plan, thanks Fleck."

Fleck shook his head. "We are not back to square one. Because we know now what they are planning. We just have to plan accordingly."

Again, I agreed with Fleck. We were far from square one. Knowing that they planned to take Nila's child was actually all we needed to know.

As a group we were resourceful, we were strong, and I was confident that we didn't need to go to Alaska.

It was a big country, we could make any place safe and a home as long we stayed together, as a group. As a family.

NINETEEN

EMPTY TRUST

Nila

February 4

A slight cramping started the night before, my belly tightened and the babies shifted, kicking a little more than usual. The difference between carrying twins, and my daughters was the movement, it was weird and often reminded me of the movie *Alien*.

I was on my rooftop watch; the snow was coming down pretty good and the contractions worried me. They weren't stopping but they weren't regular or long enough to time.

So, the first thing I did was go back to our apartment, after making sure my sniper partner was alright. After all, I lived with a doctor. Ben said to go to the medical center to get monitored.

I hated the thought of that. The days and weeks were flying by faster than I expected, and the fate of my children hung in the balance of science. If I could suspend my pregnancy in some sort of animation, to keep them from being born, I would.

I didn't want it to be labor.

More than just early labor, I knew there was a chance, even slight because of how late it was, that I would have to face Almada. It was so strained now. I wondered if she picked up on my tenseness. When Finn told me it was her idea, I wrestled with that and still do.

She never seemed fake. Maybe it really was Finn who was behind it all along, leading me to believe it was Almada and trusting that Finn would bring me my infant son instead to some lab.

My level of mistrust was through the roof, and I hated that.

The doctor on duty examined me. I felt uncomfortable, but I suppose nowhere near as uncomfortable as having Ben examine my cervix. He said it was closed tight and that was good. To be safe they strapped me down, and had me hooked up to a monitor, just like the days when the world was normal. The whoosh, whoosh of the steady heartbeats was comforting. Being relaxed and not sitting low on a rooftop felt better and while my belly still tightened, the cramping feeling did decrease.

After about an hour Almada came in carrying a small container.

"I heard you were here." She smiled and stepped in.

"It's late, I didn't expect to see you."

"I wanted to check on you and I checked in with Doctor Peters. He said you aren't dilated."

"That's a good thing."

"It is. Plus, I spoke to Doctor Rosen who said Braxton Hicks can be intense with multiple births. A half of glass of red wine wouldn't hurt."

I partially smiled. "Is that him or you?"

"That would be my mother," she said. "I remember when my sister was expecting, and she'd get those false

107

contractions. My mother would push the wine. Medically speaking the alcohol would work on slowing contractions."

"Really?" I asked.

"Well, sort of. Back before there was Magnesium Sulfate, they used to use a form of ethanol. Which is actually alcohol. I'm rambling. You're probably very stressed."

"I am."

"And if you're hungry." She set the container on the table. "I brought you curry."

I didn't know how to handle that moment. She brought me food, smiled, was gentle, there was no way that this woman wanted to take my child. Lev always said I had bad gut instincts and trusted the wrong people. I did, ever since I was a teenager, but Almada ... she was convincing.

"Thank you," I told her. "I will enjoy this very much tonight."

"It will work out, Nila."

"I just don't want to have them too early," I said. "But a part of me really thinks they're coming soon."

"Oh gosh, I hope not too soon. We have two weeks until Doctor Rosen comes and I'm leaving next week. So, prayers that they don't come in that week."

"Where are you going?" I asked.

"I want to be ready with the other scientists in Maryland. We're preparing everything for the samples."

My heart skipped a beat, just hearing Maryland, testing and scientists. "If you're there, how are you getting the samples?"

As if I didn't know the answer.

"After the babies are born, they are going to pack Baby A… I'm sorry, Baby A's placenta along with cord, and a team will bring that immediately to me. Then after he is cured and we are certain of that, his blood will be transported to us as well."

"So, you have everything ready to go, teams picked. I hope you trust whoever is bringing it to you."

"I hope I can," she replied. "But I'm not in charge of that so I don't know who it is. I'll let you get ready to get out of here." She tapped my ankle. "Take it easy, and that…" She pointed to the container. "Is still warm."

"Thank you."

"Goodnight, Nila."

"Night."

When she left, the container of her homemade food next to me, I was even more confused about her. I just didn't know how or what to think. A part of me wanted to say, 'screw it' and tell her what Finn said, but another part thought it was a mistake.

I would talk it out with Ben when I got back; that was my plan.

However, by the time they undid the monitors, I knew Ben and the kids would be sleeping.

Fleck wasn't.

He showed up at my room right as I was getting ready to leave. Almost as if someone called him or he had been waiting.

"This is a surprise."

"I wanted to talk to you, but Ben, Katie and the kids are sleeping," he said. "So, I thought I'd walk you back."

"Thank you."

"Are you okay?"

"Yeah, just false labor."

"Is it?"

"I hope. Almada suggested some wine."

"Booze is never a bad suggestion. Looks like food." He nodded to my container as he walked. "Are they giving doggy bags in the med bay now?"

"Funny. Almada brought it."

Fleck whistled. "Man, she is playing the trust game big time. How about Finn? He giving you anything? Wait." Fleck paused. "That came out wrong."

"He doesn't talk much to me. Sean, however, got the scoop on the safe passage to Nashville. And that no one really has been reporting anything west of Utah."

"Yeah, Finn told me that as well. That can mean three things."

"Three?" I asked.

"One, it's the same as here. Two, it's safe, or three it's worse."

"How can it be worse?"

"I don't know." He shrugged as we stepped out of the first building. "Anyhow, good news, I found a minivan in the garage of a house in the zone. Prime condition. It was parked for the apocalypse. As if it was waiting for us to find it. They get really good gas milage, bad in the snow, but you know, the babies hold off a couple more weeks, chances of snow decrease." He held out his hands to the falling flakes. "Unlike now."

"And we use that to go."

"Absolutely. I think we can sneak out in it, and no one would be the wiser. It'll be a tight fit with the dogs and babies, but it's just until we get clear of this place."

"Did you tell Ben or Sean?"

Fleck shook his head as we finished the short walk to the next building. "No, I just found it today. Which was weird."

"What is?"

"Did you say something to Katie?" he asked, opening the door to our building. "You know about cutting out of here."

"No why?"

"She said the strangest thing to me tonight when we went to see the dogs."

"She always does. What did she say?'

"Just that if we are going somewhere, can we wait. Her story is ending tomorrow."

"I thought she finished that," I said as we stopped at my door. "I haven't seen her drawing in a while."

"Maybe she had drawer's block."

That made me laugh and in turn, my belly thumped with a kick. I winced.

"Are you alright?"

"Yeah. Hard kick."

"Get some rest. Enjoy your curry."

"I will. Thanks for walking me, Fleck." I reached for the door.

"No problem. And Nila, everything will work out."

I gave him a slight smile, a nod of goodnight, and I stepped inside. It was quiet and dark with the exception of the small lantern that we used as a night light. It was set on the kitchen table, and I took my food over to it, and sat down. I turned the brightness up on the lantern to see my food and read whatever historical newspaper Ben was reading currently.

It was just a paper from 1955. It would be interesting to read.

By the dim light I had trouble seeing the words but enjoyed the pictures and my food. Looking at only the photos made me think of Katie and her picture book. I would ask her in the morning about it.

Following medical advice, and despite the fact everything in me said that it wasn't that sound, I drank a half a glass of Ben's wine. Actually, I downed half a glass of wine, as if it were whiskey. It was good.

I stayed up for a little longer, then washed up and went to bed. I still felt a little off, probably my nerves or the fact that that little bit of wine went right to my head. When I went into my room, Katie was sleeping peacefully on the bed, on her side. I crawled in snuggling next to her, taking in the scent of my child as her hair brushed against my nose, and I stayed that way until I fell asleep.

TWENTY

EMPTY BED

Nila

February 5

The wine worked or at least did what Almada intended it to
do. It helped me to relax and rest. It was the best night's sleep
I had in a long time. I slept hard, not once did I wake up,
and no dreams. For the first time in weeks, I felt good and
not restless.

I woke in the same position that I was in when I fell
asleep, even my arm was still extended. Only now the spot
was empty. Katie was up and out of bed.

I sat up to allow myself to get in tune with my body. No
cramping or tightness. Just normal baby kicking.

Our bedroom was made with false walls, and the only way
to tell it was day was by the amount of light that crept off the
top of the wall through the space between the wall and the
ceiling. It wasn't a lot, and the room was still pretty dark.

I could smell coffee and hear the crinkle of paper.

Ben was up probably in the sports section of his 1956 *Ev-*
ans City Journal.

I didn't hear the kids though, which told me it was after
nine and they were in class.

I turned on the light and got dressed. As I went to leave the bedroom, I noticed Katie's book. It was on the dresser, her crayons packed neatly next to it, but on top was a folded piece of paper with Fleck's name written on it.

I thought about peeking but withdrew my hand. It was Fleck's note.

The coffee smelled fresh and that called to me more than my curiosity over that letter.

Ben was seated in his usual spot when I walked out. "Kids at school already?"

"Yeah, they went about an hour ago."

"Did you let them walk themselves today?" I asked as I poured a small cup of coffee. The school was in the same building where we lived. Actually, down the hall and to the left fifty feet. Twelve students all different ages. Ben was like the helicopter parent. Walking them every day, saying each time that it was the last time.

He glanced up from his paper. "No."

"Good."

"I did watch them though until they turned the bend."

"Baby steps. Did you go peek to make sure they made it?" I asked.

"I wanted to. But I kept hearing your voice in my head."

"Ah, no worries. After my coffee, I'm gonna pop down and see Katie since I didn't get to say goodnight and she was up and out when I woke up."

"Thank you. That'll make me feel better," Ben stated. "The worry wart in me keeps thinking they didn't go."

"They went. Did you make sure they had coats in case they go outside?"

"Yes. Of course, Katie is never without that pink jacket. How are you feeling?"

"Good. No pain or tightness. Just normal pregnancy crap."

Ben chuckled at that. Not sure if he found it funny or was being polite.

We talked while I finished my coffee, nothing serious and we laughed about an ad in the paper. A Martell Brandy ad featuring a cartoon, drawn pack of cigarettes, cooking tips and recipes.

It was actually awesome but the tip for keeping things cool without a fridge was a good one to remember.

By the time I was ready to go, and I was washing my cup, it was snowing again.

Snow was safety to me. A good sign. The deaders barely moved. Not that we worried about the deaders much inside of The Colony.

When I realized it was ten, I rushed out. I knew they had lunch then recess and I wanted to pop in on Katie before her favorite time at school.

Just before I turned the bend in the hall, I heard the laughter of children and the teacher's voice. I couldn't make out what was said, I thought it was about Ronald Reagan but probably not.

I arrived at the open classroom door and prepared to knock when the teacher spotted me.

"Can I help you?" she asked.

"I'm sorry to interrupt. I just wanted to see my daughter, Katie, for a moment."

I leaned into the classroom and at the same time the teacher said that Katie was absent, I noticed she wasn't in her usual seat.

I didn't worry.

Not at that second.

I asked, "What do you mean? She did come to class, Ben watched them walk down the hall."

Then before the teacher replied, I saw Sawyer's face.

It was as if he didn't want to look at me.

"Sawyer, you walked with Katie. Where is she?" I asked.

He was so reluctant to answer.

"Sawyer," I said stronger. "Where is she?"

Sheepishly and fearful he replied, "She went to see her dog instead of coming here."

I was instantly livid on all levels, what in the world was my daughter thinking? I thanked the teacher, stepped back, and saw how Katie had done it. To my right, at the other end of the hall, was a door.

Katie probably told Sawyer she'd be back and kept on walking down the hall and straight out. Opting to not get my coat, I marched for the door. As I pushed it, Fleck was opening it.

"Where are you going?" he asked.

"To the dog area."

"I just came from there. Max is pissed, I need to get Katie back with the dog. She told him ten minutes. I can't believe the teacher let her have Caesar…"

Fleck's voice faded behind the blood rushing in my ears and my heart that beat so hard and fast I could hear it. He was saying something, I couldn't make it out.

Lost in my thoughts and immediate panic.

"Oh my God," I choked on the words. "Fleck she's not in class."

"She has to be," he said. "She took the dog. Where did she go?"

I didn't have an answer. I didn't know where she went. The only thing that kept me from losing it completely was that we were in The Colony. She was around somewhere, we just had to find her.

TWENTY-ONE

WHERE IS KATIE?

Fleck

It never dawned on me that Katie was anywhere else but in that school with that damned dog. When Nila told me she wasn't there, my first reaction was it had to be a mistake. Where else would she be? It was only a little over an hour. Max was certain that was where she went.

"Look in the building," I told Nila. "She has to be here somewhere. Call the dog, listen for the bark. I'll go back to the dog room. She's somewhere here."

"No shit, Fleck, but where?"

"We'll find her." Leaving Nila standing at the door, I spun and raced back to the dog area.

What did he tell me? What did Max say? Did I hear him wrong?

"What do you mean she's not at the school?" Max asked almost angrily.

"What did she say to you exactly?"

"She was taking him to school."

"So, she used those words?"

"Not exactly. She came and asked if she could take Caesar. It's her dog, so yeah. But I asked her wasn't she supposed to be in class, and she said yes, that was why she had to hurry."

I grunted softly. "So, she never said to you she was taking the dog to class."

"I just assumed."

"Not your fault, we all assumed Katie would be normal and go to school," I said.

"Well, she couldn't have gone too far. Everything is guarded or fenced in. Do you need help looking?"

"I might need my dog for that, I'll let you know."

Outside of the dog room, I stopped to gather my composure. I had this weird anxiety feeling creeping up my chest. I had to think, she couldn't have gone far. Still, she was a little kid, what if she fell or got hurt?

No. No.

Caesar was an amazing dog, if Katie was hurt, he would have found someone.

Hopefully, she was just hiding and playing with the dog.

The answer was getting people to search outside, the problem was I didn't really talk to anyone. Making friends wasn't on the top of my list and I worked alone. Maybe a nod or wave to a fellow deconstruction worker, but that was all.

Sean knew people though, so I went back to the building to find him.

I didn't have to go to his apartment, Nila had already got him.

Of course, she did.

They were standing in the hallway when I returned.

"Anything?" Nila asked.

"No." I shook my head.

"I'll head to the radio room," Sean said. "Start calling out. I mean, someone had to see a girl in a bright pink jacket with a dog. She can't be that hard to spot. There's only like a couple dozen kids in The Colony."

Nila folded her arms right to her body. I could tell she was so anxious but trying to look and act strong. She shook her head. "No one is gonna pay attention, Sean. This is like a small town. During the day everyone is out, and the kids take recess right outside."

"I'm gonna go check anyhow." Sean put his hand on Nila's shoulder. "It's not gonna hurt to radio out. She probably darted into a vacant store to play with Caesar. I'll be back."

Nila nodded and said, "Thanks."

I watched Sean walk away. Radioing those on post was a good call, it was their job to keep an eye out.

"What do we do?" Nila asked. "Where do we look first?"

"We go building by building."

She rubbed her face. "I have to tell Ben. He's going to be so upset with himself. This is the first day he let them walk to class alone."

That caught my attention. "Really?"

"Yeah. I joked with him because it was just down the hall and he let them go."

"It's kinda funny that she did this the first time. Like she was waiting for him to stop looking."

"That doesn't sound like Katie."

"Yeah, it does, Nila. She's sneaky and smart but there's also one other thing she is."

"What's that?"

"She's lazy. The only time she runs is with the dog and that's because she's chasing him. She lays around and draws. If the world hadn't ended, she'd be that kid on a tablet lounging on the sofa ten hours a day. If it's not art or that dog she's uninspired and that's what makes this so baffling to me. She doesn't have it in her to plot a hide and seek day."

Nila gasped. "Oh my God do you think someone took her?"

"No. Something inspired her to do it. Maybe we need to talk to Almada."

"My mind is so frazzled I didn't even think to go check with her. Maybe she's there."

"Maybe," I replied. "If not then maybe Almada knows. Katie can't keep her mouth shut. We ask the kids in the class too. She told someone about this."

At that second, I knew I had said something right because Nila's eyes widened, and she got this look of realization on her face.

"What?" I asked.

She looked at me. "The note."

TWENTY-TWO

THE KATIE TRAIL

Nila

I didn't really explain to Fleck what I meant about the note, I just raced back to the apartment with him on my heels.

Ben was startled when we walked in, he immediately stood. "What's going on?"

I didn't reply, I just went into the bedroom and could hear them talking.

Fleck replied, "Katie's gone."

"What?!" Ben blasted. "What do you mean?"

"Left. Gone. Somewhere in The Colony. She took advantage of you giving them freedom."

"Oh my God, what have I done?"

I came from the bedroom with the artbook and folded note with Fleck's name on it.

"Nila, I'm sorry. I'll help you guys look," Ben said. "She can't be far."

"I know," I replied, setting the book on the coffee table and I handed Fleck the paper. "I saw it this morning. I thought maybe she wanted you to be the first to read the book. But when you said she had to tell someone, this came to mind. Maybe it's nothing."

Fleck took the paper and unfolded it.

"What does it say?" I asked.

Fleck read it, "*Fleck, I went to finish my story. Don't worry I have Caesar.*" He folded it. "I *think* it's Caesar, anyway. She spelled it wrong."

Ben asked, "Do you know what the story is about?"

"Yeah, sort of," Fleck replied. "It's about this family in the woods, I thought it was us, but she didn't say what happened to them. Actually, it looked like a happy story, unlike other Katie drawings."

"But you never saw the end," Ben said. "She was secretive about that."

Fleck exhaled. "She said she was going to be the hero. She wants to find this family and help them."

"Why would she only tell you?" I asked him.

Very assuredly, Fleck lifted that artbook. "Because she wants me to find her."

"Why you?" I questioned.

"Because I picked up things in this book, I saw them. Now I realize they were clues." He took the book over to the kitchen table. "Ben, go find Sean. He's at the radio room, tell him we need someone from Oil City, someone that knows this area."

"I'm on it." Ben didn't hesitate, he hurried from the apartment.

I watched Fleck sit down with Katie's book of art. With each step I took towards him, I grew more scared. "You don't think she left The Colony, do you?"

"She needs to find this family."

"In The Colony?"

He only looked up at me as he turned a page, studying each picture.

"You do." I gasped. "You think she left. How?"

Fleck shook his head. "It's Katie. But I think if we figure out which direction she went, we can figure out how and if she left The Colony."

He had to be wrong. I prayed he was wrong.

There had to be no way Katie could just walk out of The Colony with her dog.

I had to believe she was still within the confines of the fenced in area, because it broke my heart to think about my child out there, alone, walking in a cold, dead world.

Although I didn't want to believe it, I never had a doubt that my daughter had a gift. She knew things, said things, and drew things that all came true. Her artbook, months in the making, was something big to her. Possibly her biggest vision of all.

Fleck shook his head. "She didn't disappoint."

"What do you mean?"

"Her twisted, dark, psychic visions," he explained. "Story is a family. Man, woman, boy and girl. Looks like they broke down or wrecked in this brown truck." He pointed to the picture. "They left it and walked. It looks like a trail. Basically, the story is they went to this house, there's others there, you can see them in the background. Then they all die. But there's blood. End of story."

"She said she was the hero in the story. Where is she?" I asked.

"She didn't draw herself, because I think Katie was going to stop this ending from happening."

"Who are these people? Are they real?"

"I think we can assume they are."

124

The door opened abruptly. Sean, Ben, and another man in his thirties came in.

"This is Piper," Sean introduced him. "He's lived here his entire life."

"I know the area well," Piper said. "Biked, four wheeled, not much I don't know. I brought a map." He handed it to Fleck.

"Awesome." Fleck took it and laid it out. "I don't know what Sean told you, but trust me when I tell you this little girl draws things that come true. We think she went to find this family. There are two clues, I think." He showed him a picture. "This truck and..." He flipped a page. "This gas station sign, which looks like you can see it in the distance."

"The truck," Piper said. "I don't know about. The Sunbeam gas station is in Rouseville. But it's not a big sign and it's old. Rouseville is here." He pointed on the map. "Three miles from here. Nothing is there. I was on a sweep team there."

"Any houses in the hills that may see the sign?" Fleck asked.

"See it?" Piper shrugged. "Hard to say. There are two spots where the elevation is high, so maybe. There are houses and cabins up there for sure." Both areas he indicated on the map. "That whole area is rough terrain. Some drops are as much as fifteen hundred feet."

"But roads go up there, right?" asked Fleck.

"Yeah."

"So, wherever the truck is, there's a trail or something. That cabin can't be far from that truck."

I was listening to them going back and forth, I don't think either of them were thinking about a six-year-old girl walking alone out there.

"It's snowing," I said. "She could be hurt."

Sean spoke up. "The snow is also a good thing. We can follow her tracks if she did get out. But how? How did she get out? There's no way."

I watched Fleck guide his finger down the map toward Oil City and he groaned, huffed and closed his eyes. "That area is behind the deconstruction zone. If she went out, that's where she went."

All I could mutter was, "Oh my God."

"She couldn't cross that creek," Piper said. "She had to take the bridge. Either Seneca or the railroad bridge."

"Let's go look." Fleck grabbed the map. "I am going to grab my gear and other things. Ben." He tuned to Ben. "I'd go to the med bay, get ready for us. Sean, you and Piper get a vehicle and radios. If she didn't stay on the road, I'll follow on foot, you guys take the road and look for the truck."

"Which road?" Sean asked.

"We'll find out when we see those tracks." Fleck faced me. "Nila, I will—"

"Don't even think about it," I cut him off. "I'll grab my gear as well. I am looking for my baby."

Fleck didn't argue with me, there wasn't time for that.

Katie already had a ninety-minute head start.

I just hoped with everything I was that she was still in The Colony.

I was in such a state of heartbroken defeat when I saw Katie's little footprints, along with Caesar's in the snow. They went

126

from the deconstruction area straight through an area that was unprotected by a fence.

We all followed them. She stayed close to the fence, past where the deaders had been a few weeks before. Their bodies frozen on the ground and footprints just walked right by them.

She took the railroad bridge. When we realized she had done that, Sean went with Piper for the Jeep, leaving us with a radio.

Piper said there was a Dollar General at the other end of the bridge. We would meet them there.

I was fearful with every step across the bridge, praying that the trail continued, and my daughter didn't slip and fall into the water below.

The snow stopped falling steadily, a flake here and there, not enough to cover her tracks. That was a good thing.

At the Dollar General we saw she made a right, staying on the road.

I kept thinking about how cold it was, how empty and deadly a place my daughter had ventured out into.

Never in my life had I felt so desperate. I watched my oldest daughter die, but I knew it was coming. This was the unknown. I was probably more scared than Katie.

When Sean and Piper arrived, Fleck and I walked ahead, following the tracks as they moved slowly behind us.

She walked about three hundred feet before making a left and crossing the train tracks again on a road called Union Street. Not long after that, she made another left, then a right.

We followed, but Sean called out for us to stop.

Did he see something we missed?

We turned around.

"Piper said this is a dead-end street. It doesn't go anywhere," Sean told us. "There's a house up there, though."

I looked at Fleck. "I didn't see a truck."

"Me either, let's check it out."

It didn't take much walking for us to know Katie wasn't headed toward that lone house. Just before the driveway to the home, Katie veered right and went into the woods.

"Okay, Sean," Piper said. "You back track with the jeep. She went right, which means she's walking parallel to Union. If there is a truck, it's on Union Street. You and Nila go—"

"No," I said strongly. "No. You go with Sean in the jeep. You know the area. We're going to follow her tracks."

"Nila," Fleck said. "Is that a good idea? I mean you're—"

"A mother who wants to find her child."

"Okay." Fleck nodded. "Sean, radio check." He lifted the radio and pressed the button. "Check."

"Got you." Sean checked his then backed up. "We'll take the road. Stay in touch."

Fleck nodded and looked at me. "Ready?"

"Yes." I nodded and took a deep breath. A few steps into those woods and following that trail, I felt my stomach tighten and a slight twinge of pain. Just a slight.

It had to be my stress causing it, that had to be it and I couldn't worry about it. I had to stay focused.

I had to find my daughter.

TWENTY-THREE

THE KATIE MISSION

Nila

Fleck did most of the talking and even he didn't say much. It was difficult, the walk was uphill, and we both were winded.

Me more than Fleck, I was walking for three people and my belly was feeling it.

I knew I had to pace myself.

It was taking a while.

We kept in contact with Sean who made it miles on Union Street without spotting a truck. He and Piper were taking other roads, side and country roads to see if they spotted it.

Piper said there were many little roads that all led to the same place.

Fleck, Katie and I just were taking the more scenic and difficult route.

Coming back down would be easier, although more dangerous. To the west of us was a drop off that at times was so steep it was frightening. We stayed the course, right behind Katie's footprints. I begged internally with everything I had for those footprints not to stop. As long as we saw them, Katie was still moving.

I didn't understand that.

How was she still going? It never looked as if she stopped, her trail was steady.

How long had we been walking?

An hour maybe. All I knew was it had been two hours since my child had been in the elements.

I could feel the burning in my legs with each hilly step I took. My muscles were pulling, and every time my stomach tightened, there would be a hard kick.

One hit me so bad, it ricocheted into my groin and down my leg. I had to stop. Leaning forward, hands to my thighs, I took a second to catch my breath.

"Are you alright?" Fleck asked, walking over to me.

"Baby kicked. It hit a nerve."

"Must be Baby Lev, he was always hitting my nerve."

Through my winded breaths, I laughed and that threw my breathing off again. Trying to settle my fast-beating heart and get a grip to get moving, I heard it.

Instantly, it rejuvenated me.

A bark.

Fleck heard it too.

I stood up straight and sure enough I saw a hint of her pink jacket.

"Yell, for her please," I said. "I don't have the wind."

"I'll do better than that. I'm getting her." Fleck took off running. "Katie!"

Katie didn't stop.

For a second, a split second, I worried. What if my daughter was bit and turned? Then when that fear hit me, I swiped it away remembering that she was immune.

I kept my eye on Fleck as I walked, because I was certain he kept his eye on Katie.

Another twenty feet and he called out that he had her. That was enough, I picked up the pace.

Four steps into my stride, I felt a sharp pain. Nothing long, nothing so intense, but it was odd. A pain, tightness, a kick.

I paused and kept going.

When I arrived at them, Fleck was crouched down to Katie's level. While Katie stood there bundled in her pink parka, holding Caesar on a leash. Her face was red from being cold.

"Katie, oh God." I rushed to her, grabbing her. "What are you doing? What were you thinking? I was scared to death."

"I'm sorry, Mommy, I left a note."

I glanced up to Fleck, who lifted his radio. "Sean, we found her, she's fine. Look for the truck, if you don't find it, we'll meet you at the bottom."

"Roger that, thank God, she's okay," Sean replied.

"Mommy, I left a note," Katie repeated. "Please don't be mad."

"I'm not mad. We'll talk about this later." I stood straight. "Right now, let's get you out of these woods and warm." I grabbed her hand, and she pulled it away.

"No."

"Katie."

"No, Mommy no. It's right there." She pointed and spoke so desperately. "They're right there. We have to go. We have to hurry. Please, Mommy."

"Katie, what are you talking about?" I asked.

"The family. We have to go before it's too late. They're right up there." Her eyes glassed over. "We have to,

Mommy. If we don't, we won't be able to save my brother. Please," she begged, "it's the only way."

Fleck looked at me. "The family in the pictures."

"We're so close. It's right at the top. You need this, Mommy. We need to do this."

My child sounded so grown up, so desperate. "How do you know it's close?"

"Nila," Fleck chuckled. "Come on, it's Katie. It's close."

I looked at Fleck and then Katie. "Okay. Let's do this. Radio Sean and tell him we're checking it out."

"Thank you." Katie hugged my legs.

"I can't make promises, Katie," I said. "I saw your drawings. We may be too late."

"Not for the boy. Not yet." Katie tugged the leash and started walking ahead of us.

"Who?" I hurried to follow. "Who is the boy?"

Katie paused for only a second, looking over her shoulder to answer me. "Lev's son."

TWENTY-FOUR
HIDDEN SURPRISE

Fleck

It wasn't Katie's fault. She wasn't deliberately misleading Nila or me. I honestly believed that she believed it was Lev's son up there. Maybe a part of her innocent mind wanted it to be true for her mother, give her something of Lev again, not understanding that Nila carried part of Lev in her womb.

Did I honestly believe our gifted psychic child was right about an unknown offspring of Lev magically living a mile or so from us?

No.

But I did believe there was a family in trouble and Katie was moved to help them.

She was right about one thing, the cabin home was at the top of the hill. Another five-minute walk and we arrived.

It was quiet and I knew all wasn't well.

No one was around, no sounds.

Bloody footprints in the snow told me whatever happened, happened fairly recently considering the snow was falling just a few hours earlier.

Nila grabbed a hold of Katie, telling her to stay close and I told them to watch for deaders while I checked inside. I didn't think there were any deaders, because Caesar would have been going nuts. He sensed them even when they weren't seen.

I was pretty certain of what I was going to find. Something inside that replicated the child drawings in Katie's book.

Footsteps all through the snow, tire tracks, two small campers and a tiny greenhouse. There was more than that four-person family that lived on the grounds. They were like us at the cabin only without the fences.

There was no blood on the porch or near the door. I grabbed my pistol and hatchet. Using the handle of the hatchet, I knocked once on the door and it opened.

Nothing came for me, and I didn't hear anything, so I went in.

It wasn't a big place; it was set up much like our cabin. An open concept idea and what I saw was worse than Katie even imagined.

In the reclining chair was a man, a rifle dropped between his legs, he had taken his own life. His body hadn't even begun to get that rotten smell and the blood still glistened.

There was a body on the couch, it was covered, blood seeped through where the head would be. Another body, a small one was on the floor, a blanket over him or her. It was a child and even though I couldn't see the body, the sight made me sick.

A pool of blood was on floor under the midsection and legs. The blankets saturated in those areas along with the head.

I moved from that to look around. The back window and door were both busted. The entire kitchen area was destroyed. Near the small hall was the body of a rager, I could tell by the veins and knew what had happened.

Someone in the camp had turned. The man in the chair took care of those he loved and then opted out himself.

I understood.

Standing there in the silence, I nearly jumped from my skin when my radio hissed. I wasn't expecting that.

"Fleck, come in."

I took a breath and lifted it. "Yeah, Sean."

"Found the truck," Sean said. "It was off the road parked on a driveway. Looks like there is a trail."

"Roger that. One of you take the trail, we'll start making our way down. Hopefully you have a short cut."

"So, you found it?"

"We found it. It's a dead camp. See you soon." I placed the radio back on my belt, finished looking in the other two rooms, then headed out.

When I walked out, I shook my head at Nila, and walked toward her and Katie.

"Nothing?" Nila asked.

Again, I shook my head. "No deaders, no ragers, no one...alive."

Katie wept out a, "No. You have to look some more."

"I'm going to check the campers," I replied.

"Then we have to go," Nila said. "We need to get you warm, Katie, and I'm not feeling well."

"Are you alright?" I asked Nila.

"I will be."

"But Mommy, he's here," said Katie. "I know it. Fleck missed him."

"Maybe whoever you're looking for is in the campers. We have to check them and see if someone needs help," I told her.

"He's *here.*"

"Who?" Nila asked.

Then Katie smiled and pointed. "Him."

"Please help me," the boy voice called out. "Don't leave me, please."

I turned around and nearly fell over.

A young boy raced to us. He was big but had an essence of young child. He was scared and came from the cabin. How did I miss him?

More than that I knew that Katie was right. I knew and I didn't see how Nila didn't know.

The second I laid eyes on him, there wasn't any doubt.

A carbon copy.

He was Lev's son.

TWENTY-FIVE

HIDDEN DANGER

Nila

A phrase uttered by me many times seeped from my mouth the moment I saw the boy.

"Oh...my...God."

Seeing him took me back to that day I met Lev when he was ten. He didn't speak a word of English, but we were kids, and it didn't matter. The boy standing before me had his hair, eyes, stocky build, everything. Not only did I feel so bad for Lev that no one told him he had a child, I instantly fell in love with the boy.

I couldn't stop staring at him. I wanted to embrace him, get to know him, but to him I was a stranger. He was a part of someone that was a part of my life and I felt like I knew him.

"Was your mommy in there?" Katie asked.

The boy shook his head. "No, my mom died when I was a baby. That was my uncle and aunt."

"I'm sorry."

He nodded.

"What's your name?" Katie asked.

"James."

My jaw clenched and I raised my eyes to Fleck.

He must have read my mind.

"I know, right?" Fleck said. "So, we have him, Katie, you guys start walking. I want to do a quick check of those campers."

Katie nodded and spoke an innocent, "Okay."

And I felt another one of those odd sharp pains and didn't say a word.

"Nila?" Fleck called my name.

"I'll be okay."

"Good. Sean found the truck and the trail. Start walking, I'll catch up."

I don't know why I agreed, what would twenty extra seconds have been to stand there? Instead, Katie and James walked ahead of me.

We didn't make it too far before Katie abruptly stopped.

Before I could ask her what it was, she spun around, yelling, "Fleck! Don't."

Fleck stopped reaching for the camper door. "What's wrong?"

"You don't need to check that," Katie said walking his way. "Just walk with us."

"Katie, it's fine. I banged on the door. I just wanna check." He opened the door. Nothing was there. "See. It's fine." He even waited a second and took a step to go inside.

"Fleck!" Katie yelled.

Annoyed, Fleck turned around. "What?"

That was it.

Out of the doorway came a deader. One easily taken down, but Fleck didn't see him.

I know I'm fast and a great shot. But by the time I drew my weapon, lifted aimed and fired, it was too late.

The deader was right behind him and dropped with a wide-open mouth, sinking his teeth into Fleck's neck. As he withdrew his bite pulling a massive amount of flesh, I shot him. It was close, but I didn't have a choice.

Katie screamed so loud, and I raced over to Fleck.

When it happened, it was almost as if it wasn't real, Fleck barely flinched. He didn't scream or cry out. Maybe it just happened too fast.

Blood pulsing from his wound, Fleck looked at me with his 'son of a bitch' look and dropped to his knees.

"No, no, no, no," I muttered out panicked. I whipped off my jacket to put on his wound.

He shook his head. "Too late."

"No." I held it to him. "Katie."

Katie was hysterical, unlike I ever saw her.

"This isn't supposed to happen." She screamed, "It's not supposed to happen."

I took the radio from Fleck's belt. "Radio Sean, tell him to hurry."

"I can't," she wept. "I have to help Fleck."

"Katie," I said stronger.

"I'll do it," James said shyly. "I know how."

"Thank you." I handed it to him and lowered to the ground to help Fleck. I could hear him radioing for help, and I felt relieved.

Sean wouldn't be long; he was already on his way.

It was bad. Even my heavy canvas coat wasn't doing much.

"Let it go." Fleck placed his hand over mine. He was still on his knees, as if he wasn't going down on his back.

"Fleck," Katie cried. "Fleck, I have the cure. Don't worry." She tossed off her backpack and reached in.

He smiled. In his weakened state, Fleck smiled. "You stole it from Almada?"

She held up the small vial.

Fleck reached for her, his bloody hand over her tiny fingers gripping that vial. "My girl. So proud. But don't waste it on me."

"No, see, Fleck, you have to let me give you a shot. You have to. You always turn out okay in my drawings."

"You're my buddy, take care of my dog."

I could feel him getting weaker, he leaned more into me for support, the color drained from his face.

He was focused on Katie, as if she was the last thing he wanted to see as he left this earth. "You guys have been my family. I love you guys. It's been fun. Let Ben know."

"No." Kate shook her head. "Take the cure. Please, take the cure."

"It's not gonna work," Fleck told her, as his head rested on my belly. "Whoa," he whispered. "The babies are coming."

And then he went still.

His hand slowly slipped from Katie's, but she stopped it and held it.

"No, Fleck, no. Don't go," she cried out. "Please don't go. Fleck! Please. Please." She got down on her knees, her hand went to his face, and she kept trying to shake him. "Don't go. Please. Fleck. No!"

It broke my heart, I knew he was gone, it took everything I had to support the weight of his body. I didn't want to lay him down, not when he tried so hard to stay upright.

140

He was my friend and my daughter's guardian angel. It hurt to know I was there when his life slipped away but even more than that it crushed my daughter. She lost her sister, father, grandparents and even Lev. I never saw her react so painfully.

Katie grabbed onto Fleck, her arms wrapped around him tight.

The weight of both of them was too much. I could feel it, and then I saw Sean. He and Piper appeared at the line of trees at the edge of the property.

He made eye contact with me and raced over.

I shook my head to convey what he already knew.

It broke him too. They had this love hate relationship, but it was still a friend in a world with so very few people.

I hated that I had to face Ben and Sawyer along with Marsha.

This was going to be hard.

It was unexpected, I mean, Fleck was the last person I thought would go down.

But he didn't really. The wrestler in him did his best 'sell,' to look strong, stay strong.

He fought.

He lost.

We all lost.

Fleck was gone.

TWENTY-SIX

HIDDEN TRUTH

Sean

"Something's wrong," Nila said.

I didn't know what she meant, I really didn't. I had just suggested that we go get the car and bring Fleck back with us. Piper said it would take twenty minutes.

"Sean, something is wrong," she said again.

Was I dense? I had to be. I was just processing what had unfolded before me. Fleck's lifeless and bloody body was leaning on Nila. Katie was holding on to Fleck for dear life, and there was a boy, the one that radioed me, who had to be the one Katie was looking for. The boy we didn't think even existed.

Lev's son.

Though my interaction with Lev was minimal, I saw pictures, and the boy was his carbon copy.

"Sean," Nila spoke breathlessly. "Piper? How long will it take to get down to the car as…as opposed to him driving up here?"

As I started to answer, it hit me what was happening. "The same amount of time, maybe…" My words trailed in revelation. "The babies?"

She nodded. "Something is bad. Can you lift Fleck?"

I hurriedly reached for him. "Katie, you have to let go. Mommy needs help." When I realized she was blocking me from lifting Fleck from Nila, I grabbed hold of Katie. She held on to him until the last second when her hand slipped from his.

I heard her sob, and the boy told her, "I'm sorry Uncle George killed your friend."

As I reached for Fleck to move him, I looked over my shoulder. "Are there any more people in your camp that turned and aren't here?"

I looked around as I moved Fleck. I didn't see any deaders, and surely if there were ragers; they would have been on us.

"Should I run and get the car?" Piper asked.

"Yeah," I answered then I saw.

I had been through two pregnancies with my wife. I've seen the stomach move from a kick, but never had seen what I witnessed with Nila.

She had removed her coat for Fleck and even through her sweatshirt, I could see her stomach shifted violently.

"Any pressure? Pain?" I asked.

"No pressure. Pain, yes. So much. Sean," she fought back tears. "It hurts so bad."

"Stay still," I told her, and fearfully, I lifted her shirt. It was worse than what I thought it would be. I could see her stomach stretched to capacity as limbs pushed against her. Legs, arms, it looked like a wrestling match in her womb. "Piper!" I yelled out. "No time. Take the kids. We'll come back for Fleck later."

I lifted Nila into my arms; my focus was to get her down that path and to the car as fast as possible. I could carry her faster than any of us could walk, and I was sure Nila was unable to move at all.

It was just about a half-mile trail and as we took it, I don't think there was a single one of us not running.

It was out of control, I apologized repeatedly to Nila for any shaking and bumping. I felt the force of her convulsing belly against my own stomach as I carried her. It scared me. I swore I worried one of the babies was trying to claw its way out and I knew which one.

Baby Lev.

He was diagnosed infected in the womb.

Piper started running with me, bracing her stomach, it slowed us down, but I was too scared to have him not do that.

"Is she alive?" I whispered. "She stopped moving."

Piper checked. "She passed out."

"We have to hurry," I said. "We need to radio the med bay to be ready."

Piper shouted to the boy, James. "James, you still have that radio?"

"Yes, sir," he replied.

"Chanel twenty. Radio. Tell them Nila is in distress. Use those words. Tell them to be ready for the babies."

"Is that the hospital channel?"

"No," Piper replied. "That's the everyone channel. We need someone there."

The proverbial light at the end of the tunnel was ahead. I could see the end of the trail, the parked car.

We made it.

"We're good, Nila," I told her. "Hold on. Just hold on."

Once we arrived at the car, I got in the backseat with Nila and Katie. I didn't want to let go of Nila, I needed to hold her stomach. I didn't know if it would do any good at all, but I had to try.

The car ride would be five minutes tops.

"Is Mommy okay?" Katie asked.

"We're getting her help," I replied.

Everything was too much. It really was. It was all happening at once. Katie disappeared on some venture to find Lev's son. I still didn't know exactly why. But seeing the dead camp told me she had to save him.

We rushed to find her against the weather elements and Fleck was killed.

Now Nila was fighting for the lives of her and the babies.

But I realized how bad things were going for Nila when I moved her a bit from my lap and saw the blood.

It wasn't Fleck's.

It was hers.

Calling out on the 'all call' channel was Piper's first thought, it was a good thing and a bad thing. Radioing just Ben would have been best. Hindsight is a beautiful thing. Our main concern was getting Nila to the medical bay.

We not only had to face everyone with Nila's medical crisis, we had to push that to the forefront over Fleck's death which was and would be devastating for so many.

When we pulled up to the medical bay, they were waiting.

Ben, Almada and Marsha. I half expected to see Finn, but I knew he was at another colony.

While I was concerned about Nila, my mind kept racing to what Finn had told us.

This was the moment. And Finn wasn't even around.

Would it matter if Nila didn't survive?

I worried about that.

Ben rushed to the cart as I put Nila down. "We have you, Nila. We have everything ready."

"She's bleeding, Ben," I told him.

He nodded as they rushed her down the hall, calling out for IV this, a push of that, do this, and that. Terms I didn't understand.

Nila woke, sitting up and screaming like I had never heard before.

Deep and painful.

"It's ripping me apart. It's ripping me apart!" and then she passed out again.

We moved toward the operating room, I felt relieved that Ben was going to be there, in there. More secure that no punches or lies would be told.

He looked at me before going in. "Fleck?"

I shook my head.

His entire face flinched up in pain and he moved forward. He glanced back again. "You coming?"

To me that wasn't an option, but now that it was, it was where I had to be.

"Yes, yes, I am."

I had to leave Katie and James with Marsha who was probably just as much at a loss as everyone else.

My mind and heart were racing out of control.

Ben expecting me in the operating room had little to do with my friendship with Nila, and more as part of the team of protection Ben and I would be for Nila and the babies.

That was, of course, if the three of them survived.

TWENTY-SEVEN

NEVER WITHOUT LOSS

Nila

I wasn't sure what it was that caused me to wake up. It could have been a number of things. The bright lights shining in my eyes, the lack of pain, the shifting and moving of my body.

I didn't know what was going on. Once I looked around, I did.

The last thing I remembered was yelling to Sean that something wasn't right. On the ground, Fleck leaning against me, I felt the babies move in my womb as if they were some sort of force that wasn't supposed to be there.

That was all I remembered.

The flutter of my eyes brought the bright light above me. I turned my head to the left to see three IV bags, one of which looked like blood, then to my right was Sean.

A cloth curtain was set up right under my breasts and it blocked me from seeing what was going on beyond it. But I could feel it. Not pain, not much, just pressure and movement.

"Sean?" I questioned.

"They're doing a C-section," he replied. "Ben, she's awake."

"Good. Nila," Ben called out. "I'm here. I'm right here with Almada. Babies' vitals are good. Can you feel anything?"

I shook my head. "No. Just pressure."

"That's us," Ben stated. "Nila, you have placental abruption. It detached. We're good now, okay, this won't be long."

I turned my head and looked at Sean. "Baby Lev is a rager," I whispered.

"What?"

"He's infected. Almada said he would be in a perpetual state of rage until he is cured."

"Nila," Almada gently called my name. "I am ready to start the cure with Baby Earl, okay? We won't wait. Promise. First baby is coming."

"Here he is," Ben announced. "Wow, big boy for being early. Cord cut. Almada, get the warming bed."

"I don't hear him," I said panicked. "Is he alive?"

"He is," Ben told me.

Then I heard the slight whimper.

Again, I glanced at Sean. "Look at the baby. See if he has the veins."

Sean moved and looked; I saw the smile on his face. He stepped back to me. "Oh, he looks good, Nila, he looks so good. His little arms and legs are moving. I didn't see the veins."

"Then that must be Earl." I took a deep breath. "Can you go watch?"

"What?"

"Please, I can't see. Go watch."

"Nila, your belly is wide open and…You know what, I will." He squeezed my hand. "It's gonna be okay."

Sean slipped by Ben and Almada, and out of my view. I knew the curtain was standard with C-sections, at least from what I heard, but I hated not knowing what was happening.

"Baby is en caul," Ben said.

"What does that mean?" I asked.

"He's still in the sack."

Almada spoke softly. "Can you get him?"

"He's small." Ben grunted. "He's slipping from my grip. Every time I think I have him…"

"Can we break the membranes and get him?" she questioned.

"We're going to have to. It's like a water balloon."

"Does that seem like a lot of fluid?" Almada asked.

"I'm not an expert…oh, I got him."

Sean peeked around the curtain. "He's out."

"Cutting the membranes now," Ben said.

"Keep watching," I instructed Sean.

I needed Sean to watch everything. It was Baby Lev, the infected twin. The twin that would not only be in a state of rage until he was cured, but the one they were going to tell me died. Ben was there, he wouldn't let her lie to me. So much went through my mind, ridiculous thoughts at that moment when I should have been basking in the birth of the twins.

"How is he?" I asked.

Silence.

"Ben? Sean?"

No one answered, but I could hear Ben.

He mumbled, "Come on. Come on. Come on breathe. Breathe, little one, breathe. Please. Please."

I held my breath, as if it were me he was telling to breathe.

At any moment I would hear a wail. A cry, whimper, something.

Then I did. A soft cry, but shrill and almost screeching. The kind of cry I expected to hear from an infected baby.

Nevertheless, he cried.

He was breathing.

I exhaled in such relief that I started to cry as well. But why weren't Ben, Almada and Sean rejoicing at the baby cry? He breathed for Ben, he cried. Was there something wrong with him?

Surely, they would have said, "All is fine, Nila."

I tried to listen but couldn't hear what they were saying with the crying.

I knew he mentioned or called for the surgical stapler. Maybe he was just busy closing me up.

But I heard whispers. All of them.

What the hell?

One whisper caught my attention. It was Almada.

"I got it, I have to move quickly..." she said. "I'll let you."

What was going on?

The slight squeak of wheels and the baby's cry faded as if he had been taken out of the room, away from me.

Almada was taking him.

That's what she was saying.

"No, Ben, you can't let her have him," I cried out. "Ben, she'll do something. Remember what Finn said."

"Nila," Ben said softly.

Sean stepped from around the curtain, bringing a blanket up as he did to cover me.

He looked as if he had been through a ringer. His face was drawn.

I felt a knot in my throat and Ben moved the curtain, he held the baby in his arms, wrapped in a blanket.

"Nila," Ben's voice cracked.

I knew, the second I heard the sound of his voice and Sean grabbed my hand, I knew.

"I'm sorry." Ben stepped closer with the baby. "We tried. We really did. But I believe he was gone before he was born. I'm so sorry."

I couldn't speak. I was afraid to do so because I knew I would break. I only nodded and reached out my hands to hold him.

When Ben handed him to me, he was so tiny, but he was beautiful. He looked asleep and I kept hoping they were wrong, then he would wake up.

Breathe, baby, breathe.

He didn't. He wouldn't.

It was a crushing blow and holding him in my arms, I just folded and cried.

I lost another child.

TWENTY-EIGHT

LOSS OF FOCUS

Nila

I wanted to take my son to the cabin and bury him next to Lev, next to my father—his namesake—and every other person I'd lost that would have loved him beyond belief.

But that wasn't going to happen.

Neither was taking Fleck there.

I didn't realize how much time had passed in the operating room between the birth of Baby Lev, and Ben handing me Earl.

Enough time to stitch me, for Almada to take the baby, and for me to bond with a child whose laughter I would never hear, whose tears I would never wipe, and whose hand I would never feel wrapped around my finger in those first months of life.

Gone.

I finally surrendered my son to Ben after God knows how long and was moved to a room. I passed out from emotional and physical exhaustion, waking much later to darkness outside the window.

Alone.

No one had come in. Not my daughter, Sean, Ben, no one.

No one, except the nurse who helped me sit up. I didn't want to be in bed, I just wanted to sit in the chair, looking out the window.

Where was my family?

Maybe they came while I slept. It was probably easier than to face me. They were all dealing with the loss of Fleck, as was I.

Now there was one more.

My child. My baby Earl.

In that room, that dark room, I felt at the pit of my existence. Depressed and destroyed. No longer was their life in my stomach, kicking, letting me know they were there.

I had no baby to hold.

And I had no knowledge of what happened to Baby Lev. All the promises of my friends that they wouldn't let him out of their sight went by the wayside when Almada took him from the room when Ben handed me Earl.

A part of me was so angry at how it all unfolded.

I didn't even feel a connection, nor did I believe I loved the babies. As a mother, you know you will love the child in your womb, but that essence of overwhelming 'My God do I adore you' love, I thought came from the moment I first saw my child.

I realized that wasn't true. I loved Baby Earl and knew how much I did when I realized he was gone.

Yes, I was drowning in a vat of self-pity, but I deserved to feel that. I earned the right to hate the world and feel sorry for myself. My baby was dead.

In a few days, I would pick myself up.

But for now, I needed to mourn.

Then I saw her standing in the doorway.

Almada.

Almost apprehensively she stood there, a shadow with the hall light behind her.

Was this the moment she told me I lost my other baby?

She whispered, "Are you awake?"

"I am."

"I have someone who wants to see you," she said. "I'm sure you want to see him."

I had no idea who she was talking about until I watched her roll the encased preemie bassinet into the room and to me. Then Almada turned on the dim light, it was enough for me to see him.

He looked so small in there, an IV shunt was strapped to his head, little monitor pads on his chest.

"He's not jaundiced," Almada said. "But Ben has him under Bili lights. It can't hurt during treatment."

"He looks so perfect," I said. "I want to hold him so badly."

"I know. You can use the holes to touch him though. A day or two and he'll be in your arms Nila, I promise."

"How is he?" I asked.

"He's doing great. Everything is working. He's a good size preemie, and his lungs are good. We all heard that strong cry."

I reached in the holes, gently stroking his soft skin. "Are we sure this is Baby Lev?"

"Positive."

"If I didn't hear that cry, I wouldn't know he was infected. He didn't look it."

"No, he doesn't. But…"

Before she could finish, I knew what she was going to say. After holding his hand, Baby Lev almost appeared violent, swinging his hands, angrily crying.

"He still does that," said Almada. "Not as often as he was. Before you could barely touch him. Now it takes a couple minutes."

"How is he eating?"

"I just gave him his second feeding. He eats very well. I just didn't want to take a chance breast feeding."

"I understand. But he'll get better?"

"Without a doubt."

"We lost Earl, I take it Katie was the match?"

Almada shook her head. "No."

"James?"

"Yes. A perfect match. Nila, I want you to know that Ben and I are going to be around the clock caregivers until he makes it through this, and then you can care for him. No one else will be near him and no one else needs to know that he was infected."

"Thank you."

She crouched down to be at my level, grabbing my hand. "I am so sorry."

There was something about her eyes; I could see her sympathy was genuine. I felt it.

"Just know, if you need to talk, I'm here. I know what this is like, I know what you're going through." She stood up. "I'll let you sit with Lev for a bit before I have to get him back on the IV."

"Thank you."

My eyes were glued to my newborn son, and I listened as she left.

For as much as my heart was broken, in a strange way it had never felt fuller; I felt an abundance of new love for Lev.

He had such battles behind and ahead of him.

"Welcome to the world, little one." I brushed my thumb over his tiny hand. "It's not a great one, but we'll make it the best we can."

TWENTY-NINE

LOSS FOR WORDS

Sean

It was the second worst day I had experienced in this godforsaken wasteland of a life filled with dead.

The first being the loss of my wife and children. The second...

Nila is my friend.

Fleck was my friend despite what he said. We are a family, and yet again we lose members and watch our group get torn apart.

The day started out with fear when we couldn't find Katie, then filled with hope when we did.

That turned.

Crossing the crest of the property, seeing Nila holding Fleck with Katie absolutely devastated was soul crushing. Then came the births.

I didn't want to be in that delivery room, but I went. I knew as soon as Ben pulled the baby from Nila that no amount of pleading, crying or praying was going to save the child. He was gone before he was born. I could see that, and I wasn't a doctor.

A part of me believed Ben could see that as well, but he didn't want to give up.

After Nila gave birth and was moved to a room, she was sedated. We all went in to see her, hoping to be that person there for her when she woke up.

She was out.

I worried but Ben said it was exhaustion from everything she experienced, and that she would be physically fine.

Almada let us all in to see Baby Lev; he is perfect.

I wanted to go over to med bay and check on Nila as the night hours crept in, Marsha even said she'd watch the kids so I could, but I knew I had that small window of Baby Lev watching from five am to ten.

Marsha would be with the kids enough. Plus, I just wanted to hold June.

There was one bright spot to the day and that was the discovery of James.

Not Jimmy or Jim, but James.

He was instrumental in helping Katie. Although I believed she was struggling with guilt but couldn't recognize that was what it was.

Marsha kept telling Katie that the babies were coming no matter what. Her mother was having pains long before Katie took her stroll. And the same outcome would have occurred, a traumatic birth, and the loss of one of the babies.

Had Katie not found James, then Nila might have lost both babies.

I felt bad for Marsha. Her and Fleck had this quirky and cute little relationship. They both wanted love in a screwed-up world, and they found it.

Maybe that was the key to some people to make it all seem better. The rage virus, the deaders, they're all fine as long as you have that one special person.

I had love.

June, my friends, I loved them all, yet the world was still a mess. Loving people made it worse, because you worried constantly about them.

There had to be a better place.

Was Alaska really the answer to it all?

Were there really boats going there, or was it all a lie from Finn?

I didn't know who to trust, I didn't. But I did know one thing. The baby that they all wanted, the one they were going to take, had survived and we had to go somewhere.

It was the second time I heard the rumor about the west. I made a mental promise to myself that by the time Baby Lev was ready to leave an incubator, I would confirm the rumors about Alaska. If true, then one way or another, I would get us all there.

THIRTY

THE PAIN WE SHARE

Nila

February 6

The high school stadium was my view from the window, and I waited for the sun to come up, which it would in that part of the sky. I dozed off here and there, afraid to sleep, afraid to dream. I hadn't moved from the chair except to go to the bathroom. I had no motivation especially after Almada came and took Baby Lev back to the care room.

"How do you see anything out there?" Ben's voice carried in the room.

I looked over to him, giving him a sad smile. "I can't. Not yet. A part of me keeps hoping I'll see a flicker of light out there though. Maybe someone alive."

"They're there. We just can't see them." He walked over, pulling up a chair and sat across from me.

"What brings you in this early?" I asked.

"I just finished my Baby Lev shift. Sean is in there now for a couple hours, so Almada and I can get some rest. I wanted to see you awake. We all popped in while you were in that deep sleep."

"I appreciate that."

"Expect Sean in a couple hours," Ben said. "How are you, Nila?"

"Emotionally, I'm a wreck. You?"

"Same." He nodded sadly. "How about physically?"

"A little sore and stiff. But then I had a great doctor, right? You were the one that did it."

"I was," Ben replied. "As I told you before, I wasn't always a plastic surgeon. I was a pretty exceptional emergency surgeon, to be honest."

"Ben, what happened? I never asked you. But considering we're both pretty raw right now, why did you leave for plastic surgery? I mean, if you don't want to tell me—"

"No, you never asked, or I would have told you," Ben said. "I had a young girl die on me. She wasn't my first, but she was around twenty. A senseless victim of a stray bullet in a drive by. I couldn't save her, I tried, but I knew it wasn't happening. The bullet went right into her femur and severed the artery. By the time I got to her she bottomed out. It was her mother that made me quit the next day. I will never forget her mother's anguish, the begging, the praying, the asking why and pleading with me to save her. It was horrible and painful. I never wanted to be the person responsible for that."

"You weren't."

"I know." Ben nodded and grabbed my hand. "Inadvertently I did, because there was nothing I could do, but it doesn't stop the guilt. I knew in plastic surgery it would be rare to feel that way again."

"I'm glad you're as talented as you are. Thank you. And you are not the cause of my anguish."

"I know. I just wish I could have done more."

"We all do," I said.

"And we're doing everything for Baby Lev. He's gonna be good. He's strong, Nila, he is so strong. Six pounds, and eight weeks early, that's unheard of."

"Ben." My fingers fiddled with his hands. "Answer me honestly, do you think he was the reason baby Earl died. Did he kill him?"

"What?"

"He's a rager."

"*Was*. And not in the sense that we know ragers. Earl was still in the sack. Put that out of your mind. Okay?"

"Yeah," I replied softly. "When do you think we can get him in our care, with us and away from Almada. I hate that she has so much control."

Ben gave my hand a squeeze before he gently pulled back, grimaced his face a little and sat back. "You're wrong there. We were wrong about her. I don't know if Finn misunderstood."

"But Finn said she and Rosen had this plan. Almada is supposed to go to Maryland, I mean it fits into everything he said."

"I know, I was the one that questioned why Finn would lie. And I still don't have an answer to that. I mean I can't figure out why he sent Sean out in teams chasing after people who used the dead as weapons."

"Because they were a threat."

"Yes, yes, they were and are. I mean, the execution teams are doing a great job cleaning up the hoards when they find them. I just don't think they're a threat to us. And why Sean? I think it was all a matter of earning Sean's trust because he is close to us."

"Seems elaborate," I said.

"Maybe." Ben shrugged. "Something is off. And today, that feeling just deepened in my gut. Maybe it was Fleck dying, Katie being lost. Everything happening, I don't know."

"Again, Finn said they want Lev. He's going to deliver him to us and we're going to Alaska with him. I believe that."

"Okay. And I believe he's wrong about Almada. I am going to assure you that Almada wouldn't keep your child from you. She would not, could not, tell you Baby Lev was dead when he wasn't."

"How?" I asked.

"Nila, she was sobbing. I mean…I found her in a closet sobbing over what happened to you and losing the baby. She genuinely was heartbroken and vowed to save Baby Lev. It was all a bad trigger for her, reliving a horrendous time for her."

"What do you mean?"

"She told me why she was so upset, and that is the reason I believe she wouldn't do that to you," Ben stated. "Nila, Almada's story is bigger than you know. Right before the outbreak started, she was eight months pregnant. In the midst of it all, all the chaos, she went into labor and her child was still born. I just can't see her lying to add to your pain in the name of science. She's genuine, Nila, she really is."

I heard what Ben was saying and how he believed his words, but I didn't know what to believe. Almada, Finn. So many supposed versions of the truth were being thrown at me, I wasn't in any state to sort through what was true and what wasn't. Whose side I would take.

My sorrow formed an impenetrable wall that nothing could get through, and all I felt was pain. I didn't want to be in The Colony, away from my daughter, my son, all while dealing with the loss of friends and a child.

I just needed something to happen, a sign, that would give me a clear-cut direction on what to do next.

Only one thing was certain. I had to do whatever was necessary to keep my children safe.

THIRTY-ONE
THE MOMENTS WE SHARE

Nila

February 9

My son was four days old, and in the same breath it was four days since I lost my other son. I was able to walk around, not a lot and not too fast, and I was feeling stronger. Yet I stayed in the med bay; I did not want to be far from Baby Lev.

I kept being told that 'any day' we could take the baby to our apartment.

Baby Lev was better. Almada labeled him cured of the rager virus and his blood was showing astronomical immunity effect as she expected.

She was happy about that.

It worried me, though. Suddenly, my child saving the world wasn't important. I just wanted my child safe.

On the positive side, my family visited several times a day and we tried to have one meal together. Usually, a late lunch worked out best for us all.

Katie and James would always stay and hang out with me and the baby when he was allowed out of his protective bassinet. Ben would come to pick them up. Everyone was trying to help me through, but that would just take time.

I learned a lot about James in the few days since he joined us. He was a super mature eleven years old. Like Katie, he was smarter than his age. He was raised the last several years by his aunt and uncle. Before that, his grandparents. His mother passed in an accident when he was just two and all he knew of her came from a few photographs and some stories from his grandfather.

I thought at first it was my imagination that James sounded like Lev. He looked exactly like him as a boy, but he spoke like his father too. The minimal use of contractions, the perfect speech. Then just before I brushed it off as my imagining things, I realized it was true, because his entire family was Serbian, like Lev.

But unlike Lev who was adopted by English speaking parents, James was raised with the language.

His family was originally from New York and that explained it all to me. Knowing what I knew, Lev was working as an interpreter in New York. He probably met James' mother there.

James was enthralled with Baby Lev. Even more so than Katie. He enjoyed playing with his hands and staring at him. "I cannot believe this is my brother. My real brother."

"Yep," I told him. "Your brother."

"And I'm your sister now, too," Katie said.

"I always wanted a brother or sister, now I have both." James smiled.

"And cousins," Katie added. "Sawyer and June. Pap Ben. You're not alone, James."

"I miss my family."

"I know, sweetie," I told him, stroking his head. "You will always miss them. You can talk about them anytime, we would love to hear about them."

Just then Ben knocked on the door and walked in. "You two ready?"

"In a minute," Katie replied.

"Can I teach Lev the language my grandfather taught me?" James asked.

"Absolutely," I said.

"Did my father know Serbian?"

I nodded. "Yes, he did. That's probably how he met your mom."

James sighed out. "She said he died."

"She may have thought he died. Lev, your dad, was in the military reserves. He worked as an interpreter. He actually served overseas, probably about the time you were born, and there were some conflicts. She may not have known he didn't die. Just know, had he known about you, he would have been in your life. Lev was a good man."

"Why didn't she ask if he was dead?"

I shrugged. "I don't know. Maybe she tried. I know Lev was dead to me for a period of time." I glanced up to Ben when he cleared his throat. He understood my 'dead to me' reference because he knew about the turbulent post teen times.

"Okay, say goodbye," Ben instructed. "We'll see them before we go to bed." He snapped his finger a couple times and both kids darted me a kiss. "Nila, get out of that chair and go to bed please."

"I will."

"I'll check back. I'm hoping tomorrow is the day," Ben said as he gathered Katie and James.

"Me, too."

It was fast to get an eight-week-early baby out from constant care, but really, I lived with a doctor, I wasn't worried about it. If we were headed to the cabin, that would be a different story.

We wouldn't be in The Colony long.

We were slated to go to Alaska, the new world so to speak.

Ben and the children had left, and after a few minutes, I looked at my watch knowing it would be time to take Lev back to the care room. I would call it a nursery, but he was the only baby, and he was getting constant care.

I'd take a nap when the nurse came to give him to Almada.

I wasn't expecting Finn to show up at my room.

He looked, for lack of a better word, like a humbled man, fearful to come in.

"May I?" he asked.

"Yeah."

He stepped inside and immediately walked to me. He extended his hand to mine as he looked at the baby. "He's beautiful."

"Thank you."

"Nila, I...I am so sorry. I am so very sorry," he said, heartfelt. "I came as soon as I got back. Fleck...and this. It's heartbreaking."

"Thank you."

He took a deep breath and exhaled. "At least he's healthy, right?"

"He is. Better than a preemie should be."

He stared at Lev then turned to me. "I feel responsible, that we all are responsible for this tragedy."

"How?" I asked, confused.

"Karma kicking us in the butt or rather you."

"What do you mean?"

"The plan they had to tell you Baby Lev died so they could have complete control of him, like fate said if you lie about it, it happens. And he…he did."

"Finn, this—"

Finn cut me off. "I know that the plan was for you to take this baby and head to Nashville, and I would bring Baby Lev. I know the plan was for all of you to go, to follow the transport, take the plane, go to Alaska—"

"That hasn't changed."

"Good." He squeezed my hand. "Maybe going to Alaska will be a good start. A fresh start. Try to focus on healing. I'll be there. I just wanted you to know that I would get you there if you still wanted to go."

"We do."

"Two weeks. And who knows, maybe it isn't in vain," Finn said. "Maybe Baby Lev can still save the world in his own way. They did get what they could."

I was getting ready to clarify for him that all hope wasn't lost, when Almada walked in.

"Nila," Almada said. "I need to take…" she shifted her eyes to Finn. "The baby back to be under the lights."

Finn stepped back. "I'll check back. Again, Nila, I am very sorry."

I nodded sadly, and waited until he left, then I glanced up at Almada. "Did you speak to him?"

"I did."

"Were you the one that gave him the update on all that happened?"

"I was. I made sure he came to me and only me," she said.

"He thinks this is Baby Earl."

Almada nodded.

"You told him that?"

"The blood shows immunity," Almada stated. "To someone not looking deeply, this baby was born immune. No one outside our circle knows this is Baby Lev."

"Why?"

"Because Ben told me." Almada crouched down before me. "Nila, I would never, ever tell you a child died to take him for experiments. I wouldn't do that. I have all that I need."

"Ben told you?"

"He did and I am glad. I can protect you now. All of you. I have what I need from the baby. Follow the plan. Go to Alaska. Do what he says. Get as far away as possible. As long as you do, we can keep Lev safe."

"I'm so confused. If this wasn't your idea, was it Finn's?"

Almada shrugged. "I don't know whose idea. If it even was an idea. Hell, for all I know some scientist in Alaska wants Lev. But as long everyone thinks he died, everything is fine. But if it gets out, he will be sought after."

"Come to Alaska," I told her, not even thinking before the words slipped from my mouth. "Come there. Work on the cure there."

"We have what we need in Maryland, I can't guarantee they have that in Alaska."

"Almada, this is a dead world," I told her. "It's not going to get better, and you can't cure everyone. Think about it. Be with us all."

"I'll think about," she replied. "But we have a secret to keep. Tell no one. Make sure your group keeps it tight lipped."

"I will." I nodded. "Thank you. And I am sorry I doubted you."

"No, it's okay." She reached for the bassinet. "Two weeks. That's all. Once you are in Alaska, you can start to live."

Almada left the room with Lev in her arms, and me even more confused.

Who to trust? Who was telling the truth? Was it possible that they were all believing different things, or was I just purposely being misled so I handed my child over to them?

Bottom line was within the blood of my child, was the cure.

Taking off for Alaska was running away with the one chance humanity had to beat the virus once and for all.

Was I wrong for even considering leaving?

Once again, I missed my friend and longed for his advice as I pondered the question, "What would Lev say?"

I could answer that, but one day I would have to answer my own questions, solve my own dilemmas. As the clock ticked for us all, I just didn't know if I was ready to.

PART THREE

NEW HOME

THRITY-THREE

THE UNCERTAINTY WE SHARE

Sean

March 1

"Again," I told Nila, as I secured gas cans with bungee cords on the roof of the minivan. "I can tell you what Fleck would say. I kind of think Lev would say the same."

I pulled the cord, possibly putting some of my frustration into the tug. It could have been shorter, but we had to wait for a break in the weather, so for the past three weeks Nila constantly asked me the same questions.

Am I doing the right thing?

Should we be going now?

What do you think Lev would say?

I didn't really even know Lev other than what I met for a short period of time at The Colony. Lev was a presence, an overbearing and overprotective one, not to mention jealous. But Lev was canonized in Nila's mind and God help anyone who said anything negative about him.

I supposed in time that would change.

However, not even a year after his death, was just too soon.

"I guess you're right," she said.

"About?"

"What Fleck would say."

"Nila, I didn't say anything."

"Sorry."

"Look." I stepped to her. "I know this is big. Okay, the kids…" I glanced over to all four of them who stood patiently off to the side, waiting to go, even though we were still a good fifteen minutes or so from that. "They are looking forward to it, so focus on that."

Nila nodded. "Alaska."

"Yeah, in less than a week, we'll be there."

"Do you think it's safe to fly?"

"I think it's safer in the air than on the ground, but Finn assured me they have a clear route from all Colonies that are participating. They wouldn't put a hundred plus people in a plane that wasn't safe. It's a new start."

"And we're going to swing by the cabin on the way?" she asked.

"Absolutely. Secure it as best as we can." I walked around to the back of the van. The hatch was open, and the bags were inside, all military duffle bags.

I started thinking about how hard it would've been, before the world went to shit, to pack only one bag. Yet, we had no problems, and the kids actually shared one.

"All right. June's car seat is in," I said. "The base of Lev's is in, as soon as Ben gets back from med bay, we'll take off. It'll be a tight squeeze but hey, we only have twenty-three hours' driving time. Why don't I start loading up the kids, you can go get Baby Lev from Marsha?"

"I wish she was going," I said. "Almada, too."

I looked down at my watch. "Well, she's supposed to meet us here to say goodbye, you can always throw one more guilt attempt at her."

"I just might. Let me go guilt Marsha first. I'll check your apartment, see if anything was left behind that you may have missed, and then grab the baby." Nila stepped back, turned, and paused. "By the way, Sean, the weight looks good on you." She walked away.

"Thanks," I blurted out, then it dawned on me what she said. "Wait. What?" But Nila was gone, making her way into the residential building. I shook my head and looked over to the kids, they had inched their way closer to me.

I had the van parked right outside the building. I was just waiting on Ben and Nila to return with the baby. Marsha wanted to spend time with him before we left.

The trip was planned out. Finn had assured us all routes were clear and once we made it to Nashville Colony we could stop for the night.

It wouldn't be until Texas that we were reunited with the dogs. Katie wasn't happy about them going in a truck, but we just didn't have the room.

We were about to venture into the unknown, travel to a part of the country none of us had been to since things fell apart. Of course, we wouldn't see anything from Texas to Washington State.

I looked forward to landing in a place not swarming with infected, and even more so going by boat to Alaska. It would be nice to sleep, not carry a gun, or have to be prepared for the worst all the time.

Almada was confident she would have a working cure within a year. If the mainland survived that long. If it did, we could eventually return.

"Deep in thought?" Ben's voice snapped me out.

"Uh, yeah, sorry, I was. When I should have been loading the kids."

"We have time." He lifted a bag, one of two that he carried. "Medical stuff."

I took it and loaded it. "The other?"

"Oh, no that's snacks and food."

"Speaking of which. Did I get fat?"

Ben chuckled. "What? Where is that coming from?"

"Nila said the weight looks good on me."

"It does." Ben smiled and gave a swat to my arms. "I'll get the kids."

I reached down for my gut, it didn't seem big, but my pants did seem tighter in the seat. I just thought they shrunk.

"Here comes Almada," Ben said.

I glanced at my watch then back up. She did as she promised and showed up right on time. Like she always did, and it looked like she came with food.

"Travel snacks." She handed me the container. "Where's Nila?"

"She went up to sweep the rooms for missed stuff."

"Like you do in a hotel?"

"Exactly. Then she's getting the baby. Thank you for this." I walked over to the side door to put it in, when I heard Katie excitedly call for 'Almie.'

Ben snuck in by me with June. "We are going to be squished," he said while placing her in her seat.

"Tell me about it," I replied.

After placing the container in the back seat, darting a kiss to June, I heard something else.

We all heard something, each picking up on a different sound.

Gunshot? That was what I heard. Two, three, rat-tat-tat.

"Someone is screaming," Ben said.

"What is the commotion?" Almada asked.

I backed up from the van and turned toward where the sound was coming from.

"Look." Katie pointed as she slowly walked away toward the trouble. "A man on a bike is leading the deaders."

"Oh my God," I breathed, as I charged forth and swept up Katie.

She was right. They were at the entrance of our main camp, the school property. A man on a bicycle peddled down the road leading a pack of deaders. Behind them men hooted and hollered. I could hear the shots from our men ringing out. Aiming for the dead, aiming for those who brought them.

It was them. The ones I looked for on the road before the weather turned bad, the ones Ben insisted didn't exist and Nila thought weren't a threat. They waited for the weather to break.

They went big.

They came for us with a huge hoard.

I carried Katie to the van, almost like a football, and grabbed Sawyer on the way, tossing him in.

Ben urged James inside.

"Almada, in," I instructed.

"But I can't leave."

"Tough. Go. Now." I tossed the keys to Ben as Almada climbed in. "Get them out now. Worry about strapping the kids once you're free and clear."

"But the deaders, those men are blocking the entrance."

I looked at Katie then at Ben. "Katie knows the back way. Right Katie?"

Katie nodded. "The fence is down back there. But Mommy—"

"I'm getting her and your brother and Marsha. Show Ben the back way." After she nodded again, I closed the door of the van and pulled my pistol. Walking backwards, I called out to Ben. "I'll meet you on that main road by the Dollar General. If it's not safe, have Katie take you up the mountain. We'll find you."

Ben gave me his agreement and got inside the van. I spun round and raced for the residential building. Just as I hit the door, so did Finn.

"I didn't think they'd hit us, Sean," he said.

"Neither did I. Where are you going?" I rushed in.

"Making sure people get out. You?"

"Nila."

THIRTY-FOUR

HOME INVASION

Nila

When Katie first drew the picture, I laughed, but Fleck was not amused. Simply because he knew before us all that Katie had a gift. Fleck kept that picture and hung it with masking tape on his wall.

I stopped at his apartment before getting the baby to see if anything important had been left behind.

Ben had gathered Fleck's pictures from his wrestling days, and his journal, that I never knew he had written. The artwork from my daughter was left behind. Maybe Ben did it on purpose. The picture was of him bloody, being bit by a deader. Staring at it, the drawing was no longer humorous, but ominous. Fleck had kept it for a reason, and so I would too. I folded it and put it in my back pocket.

Just as I was leaving, I heard gunshots and screaming. I flung open the door to go get the baby. I knew Sean and Ben were with the other children.

There were two stairwells. One was on the east side of the building where the main entrance was located, and the other was all the way on the west side. Fortunately, our apartment was in the classroom one stairwell up and that was ten feet from Fleck's door.

I raced into that main stairwell, only to see Sean and Finn running towards me.

"Where's the baby?" Sean asked.

"Upstairs, I was in Fleck's place looking. What's going on?"

"We're being invaded," Sean said.

"By deaders?" I asked.

"Yes," Finn answered. "Led in as weapons."

"Oh my God those people are real?" Obviously, they were, and they were here. Coming for us. As I raced upstairs, I called back, "Where are Ben and the kids?"

"He took them out of the compound through the back," Sean replied. "We'll head that way. We can't go toward the main entrance."

"Jesus," I gasped. "And I don't even have a gun."

"Here." Finn handed me one.

"Thank you." I reached for the door. "Marsha!" I called out as I opened the door and burst in the room.

Empty.

"Marsha!" I called out.

"She's not in the bedrooms," Sean said.

"She must have ran," I said. "When she heard everything."

Sean shook his head. "Then why didn't we pass her on the steps. They're closest."

"How long was she up here with him?" Finn asked.

"Ten minutes," I answered. "Fifteen tops."

"What did she take?" Finn questioned.

"Huh?" I was confused. "The baby in the seat."

"No," Finn said firmly. "What did she take? Did she take anything else beside the baby?"

I looked around. "Um, the diaper bag, formula bag."

"She didn't take the baby to safety," Finn stated. "She took the baby. And I'm willing to bet she left long before the commotion."

It took a second for it to register what Finn was saying, it was then I had my 'Oh my God' moment. All the second guessing, who to trust, who was lying. I teetered between Finn and Almada, over which one really wanted to take the baby, when the person was right under my nose.

Finn said Doctor Rosen told him it was Almada.

Marsha was Rosen's daughter, she wormed her way in, gained our trust, and in return we trusted her father.

We told her everything.

Now she had taken off with my son, and The Colony was under attack.

The only positive could be that she left before the attack, meaning baby Lev would be safe. For now, anyway.

Sean flew to the door. "She went out the other staircase. She had to."

"Where is she going?" I asked. "Is she leaving or hiding the baby?"

"Leaving," Finn said. "Rosen had to have set something up. Get the baby as planned. That's the only thing I can think of."

Sean opened the door. "We need to go. She has a fifteen-minute head start at best. She probably went the same way Katie left. Through the de-con area. But you know what she wasn't expecting?"

"What?" I asked.

"Ben's out there with the kids, right behind her." Sean ran out the door and didn't wait for us.

I stopped Finn as we followed. "Do you really think it's Rosen?"

"Yeah." He nodded. "But we'll know for sure when we find her with the baby."

The marauders or whatever they were called, weren't doing some super military attack or Blitz Krieg, they weren't coming at us at all fronts, they just simply marched through the front gate, taking out all those who got in their way.

I firmly believed they didn't care if people escaped. If they lived or died, they were there for the goods. To get everything they could.

I didn't have a good idea of what all was going on.

I knew that when I left to get the baby, Sean was packing the van, the kids were waiting, and Ben was supposed to return.

Without hearing details, I guessed that Sean ran for me and the baby, and Ben took off in the van with the kids. According to Sean, Ben was headed toward the back near the deconstruction area.

Back in the day when Lev was with us, before he got sick, and before The Colony fell, there was a sense of saving. We wanted to help as many people as we could. We made our escape with others. But this time was different. Maybe because it wasn't just deaders descending on The Colony but rather a semi-calculated attack. There was no sense of camaraderie or community, at least to me, it was just about getting my family to safety.

Until I heard them.

Racing to the route that Katie had used, I moved slower than normal, bringing up the rear.

Just about at the door I heard the children from the classroom, and I stopped.

Some cried, some voices were expressing confusion. No one was screaming so there were no deaders in there.

"Nila," Sean beckoned. "Let's go."

"No, go, you and Finn move faster than me. I have to get them."

Both he and Finn walked back toward me.

"No." I stopped them. "Go find my son. I'll meet you by the Dollar General."

I hated putting the rescue of my son in someone else's hands, but I knew damn well Sean or Finn could run faster if I wasn't holding them back.

I hurried to the classroom and when I arrived, the teacher was gathering the six kids.

"We're trying to hide or get out," the teacher said.

"We have to get them out," I told her. "The Colony is under attack. Let's keep them close and follow me. "Everyone has to move fast. Okay?"

Once I got the agreement, I led them down the hall. Before turning the bend to the exit, I checked the hallway to make sure it was still clear.

We stayed in one huddled group, down the stairs and to the door. Again, I checked it out.

The sounds of commotion increased, as did gunfire.

Before leaving, I turned to everyone. "We're going to head out and run as fast as we can straight to the gymnasium building. We'll stay behind it and hit the wooded area just behind."

"Then what?" asked the teacher.

"We're getting out of here through the deconstruction zone. We'll be fine."

The path forward did seem clear, and every noise seemed to come from behind us.

The gymnasium was a parking lot distance from us, and the only time we would be in the open.

I was worried until I saw how fast those kids ran.

Some right by me. They charged forth like they were going to recess.

One little boy around nine years old was really far ahead of me. I tried to get him to stop, but I didn't want to yell, and I didn't want him running to the woods without us.

He was the first to arrive behind the gym, but he didn't go much farther. Leaping out at him, and nearly knocking him over, was Katie's dog, Caesar. He wasn't attacking, he seemed genuinely excited to see the boy, but I also knew how Katie trained him.

There had to be a deader nearby and Caesar was protecting him from it.

I was surprised to see Caesar, but even more when I saw Three-Sixteen. The dogs had broken free. Marsha asked for him, so that made me wonder if she really was stealing my child. Why would she leave behind a dog she asked for?

Perhaps I was trying to rationalize it.

As we inched safely to the wooded area, sure enough the Caesar warning system was working. A deader moved about the woods. He didn't move fast or with purpose. He was pushing the decomposing state where he could just fall apart. His jaw already hung off of his face.

One of the kids screamed at the sight of it, and it caught his attention.

"He's not a threat. We're faster," I said. "This way."

I switched places with the teacher, and I brought up the rear while she and Caesar led the way.

When we arrived at the deconstruction part of The Colony, a few deaders moved about. Again, not a threat and we could easily slip by them. There were none of the bad guys, so I didn't worry.

At the end of the cul-de-sac, fresh tire tracks cut through the mud and straight to the weak perimeter. The broken fence was pushed outward, and I hoped that was Ben and the others. A set of footprints followed in that same mud, so we did as well.

It led to the narrow road, and we took that to the railroad bridge. Muddy footprints were in the planks. No tire tracks. A vehicle couldn't cross that bridge anyhow. Ben would have had to go a bit father.

We'd all end up at the same place. That was what mattered.

I was leery about the railroad bridge that went across that creek. It was high up and left us with little options if we were overcome by deaders.

Fortunately, we weren't, and we made it across to the back alley behind the Dollar General.

It was there I realized the shots were now coming from in front of us.

How naive I had to be to believe the area around the store was clear. If the gang brought the dead through the front gate, they must have traveled that street to get there.

Probably looting their way to The Colony, leaving a few stragglers from their weaponized army of the dead.

That was when I started to really worry. If Marsha went that way, she might have walked right into it, carrying my defenseless baby.

I knew one thing for sure, though, if the deaders or raiders didn't get her, I was killing her myself.

The gunfire was systematic and sporadic, as if someone was picking off a defenseless enemy.

After telling the teacher and kids to stay tucked back against the building, I told the dogs to watch them, and I went to check it out.

I inched my way closer to the side of the building and halfway there I spotted Sean and Finn. They walked along side each other, with only a few feet between them. They were moving forward and aiming.

I picked up the pace, calling out, "It's me," as I emerged from the side of the building to the street and to Sean.

Looking to my left I saw about fifteen deaders on the ground.

"Ben?" I asked. "Have you seen him?"

"I saw the van up ahead, he turned the corner. He's fine. The kids?"

"Behind the store." I lifted my weapon to shoot and that was when I saw it.

In fact, I was pretty sure we all saw it at the same time.

As the one deader dropped, he no longer blocked the view of the car seat.

My heart sunk, and I prayed as I raced towards the car seat, that it wasn't what I thought it was.

There were other deaders on the street, but I didn't care. That car seat was my only focus.

Shots from Sean and Finn still rang out and that distance seemed so far. It felt like a dream, like I was running in slow-motion.

The infant carrier was on its side, and with each hit of my feet on the pavement, I begged, "Please no. Please no. Please no."

Did the gunfire stop or did the sound of my heart and blood in my ears drown it out?

I arrived at the car set, scared to death.

Then I saw blood on the handle. I closed my eyes, not wanting to see. But I had to…I looked.

It was empty, but there was blood in the seat.

My knees buckled and I dropped to the ground.

Oh God.

My baby. My poor baby.

My hands shook as I grabbed onto that carrier, my soul ready to scream from the depths of my pain when I heard it.

A cry.

It was weak, whimpering but it was a baby's cry. Immediately I stood. Was it one of the kids?

No.

"That way," Sean said, pointing.

"Blood trail," Finn added. "Look."

It wasn't old, it was new. A trail of blood. At points it was droplets, and other times it was small puddles.

Sean and I followed it quickly.

If my child was hurt, he was still alive. He was immune. I just needed to get him to Ben.

The blood led to a blue building on the other side of the vacant lot and the cry was louder.

A bloody handprint was on the screen door, and I could hear the baby inside.

I kept thinking, what if it wasn't Baby Lev?

I tried for the door, but it was locked. I stepped out of the way to get something to break the window, and when I did, Sean slammed against the door.

His determination fueled a strength and after three rams against that door, it popped from the lock, splintering the frame.

We didn't have to look far.

Marsha was on the floor, half sitting as she leaned against the couch for support.

She was covered in blood and holding my son.

Immediately I lunged, taking the baby from her, fearful of looking at how badly he was injured.

So much blood.

As I gently took him, I realized it wasn't his blood.

It was Marsha's.

A bite to her neck and her arm, both deep with flesh torn from her.

I quickly looked at Lev, examining him. I saw nothing and handed him to Sean. "Please check him. Make sure I didn't miss anything."

When Sean took him, I stared at Marsha.

She breathed heavily, her eyes blinking fast. "Deaders. I got him away. I protected him."

I would have praised her efforts and thanked her, but I had to know. "Did you take the baby to protect him from the attack on town?" I asked.

She stared for a moment, then repeated herself. "I protected him."

Sean whispered, "Baby Lev is fine. No marks. No bites."

Again, I asked her. "Why did you take the baby?"

"I protected him."

"Marsha."

"The world needs him. There weren't supposed to be deaders," she cried. "There's a truck waiting."

I felt my heart thump in the pit of my stomach. "You stole my child."

"You can't take him, Nila. You can't take him away. He's the only hope." She cried more, trying to catch her pain filled breaths. "We need him, Nila. If you take him to Alaska, we won't survive."

"If I don't take him, *he* won't survive," I said. "There's no choice. Not for me."

Marsha whimpered.

"Take the baby outside, Sean, please." I kept my eyes on Marsha. When I saw through the corner of my eye that Sean had walked away, I raised my gun and aimed.

Before I could depress the trigger or hear anything more that she had to say, she began to twitch. Her head shook with rigid movements, and I realized what was coming.

Within seconds she would be a rager. And with a single shot, I stopped that from happening.

THIRTY-FIVE

WHAT IS HOME

Sean

Nila was beside herself, and while she tried to put on a bold front, I saw it. The pacing, the occasional stopping to catch a breath.

By the grace of God, Baby Lev survived.

Ben and the others waited on the side road, a steep hill the deaders had a hard time navigating.

Finn and I had cleared the street of danger. No longer was it just our family, we now had Almada, Finn, six more kids, a teacher named Amy, and my teammate Steve, who made it out the same way we did.

Eighteen of us and eleven were children. The oldest was only twelve and the youngest was the baby.

We had a minivan and we needed to get out, get far away from The Colony and to safety.

"Do you know how many?" Finn asked Steve. "Did you get to see how many?"

"Deaders?" Steve replied. "Too many to count. The raiders or looters, or whatever you want to call them, maybe two dozen."

That caught Nila's attention. "Two dozen and they're taking over the entire Colony? Why can't they take them out?"

"Because we were saving people," Steve replied. "There was no room for me on the truck and I hightailed it out of the deconstruction area. They went another way."

"Any radios?" asked Finn.

Steve shook his head.

Ben spoke up. "Why don't we find a way to get to the cabin? We were headed there anyhow. Let's regroup, let the kids settle. It's secluded and we have that radio stashed there. It's a good spot."

Steve questioned Ben, "How are we going to power it?"

"Solar generator," Ben replied. "It's tucked and hidden on the other side of the fence in the woods, in case someone came."

Finn nodded. "Then we go. But how?"

I stepped forward and peered down the hill back to where we had just left.

"There's a lot of cars down there. If I'm not mistaken, I saw a car repair place not far from the store. We get everyone safe inside somewhere and we look."

We packed as many kids as we could into the van, drove it back down and parked it behind a bar called Rusty's.

The windows had been boarded up, the metal front door had a lock on it, and it surprised me that no one had busted in there. I too would have thought it was an old, abandoned business had it not been for one of those folded signs that businesses prop out front. The sign for Rusty's lay on the sidewalk. The writing had long since worn off, but it was there.

We cut the bolt, I checked inside, it smelled old and dirty, but there were no deaders.

It was a safe place for Nila, the kids, and Ben to wait while we went and searched for working vehicles.

They had to get us the hour drive to the cabin, and then we could figure out our next steps from there.

I felt confident, having been on the team tracking the raiders, that we wouldn't run into them. They made their way west after Evans City into the bordering towns in Ohio and they were looping back.

To me, they had been looking for the Colonies all along, and probably found us a lot sooner than they hit us, but they knew deaders were useless in the bitter cold and using ragers was dangerous all the way around.

They hit the jackpot with The Colony, they would stay and not move until they'd used everything we had, like locusts.

From what we saw, that's what we deducted. I remember trying to talk to Ben about it once and he still never believed it.

I guess that changed.

After two hours, which really pushed my anxiety levels up, we found two vehicles and squeezed them all in.

Our family—me, Ben, Nila, and the kids—rode in the van. Nila sat up front with me, taking turns with Ben holding the baby. That made me nervous, no car seat.

What could we do?

Nila said she was certain there was a car seat in the lost and found at Big Bear.

No one had been there since Nila poisoned the well.

A story that would haunt her the rest of her life. Not that she felt guilty, she didn't. But no one would ever let it rest.

Fleck especially.

We made it without incident to the road that led to the cabin, and were nearly at the top of the hill, when I saw the straggling deader. I knew something was wrong. They just didn't randomly make their way there.

When we reached the hill's crest, my suspicions were confirmed.

The gate had been knocked down, and the front door to the cabin was wide open. The shutters were still closed but it was obvious someone had been, or still was, inside.

Someone had raided the cabin and I was willing to bet by the sight of the eight deaders, that it was a faction of the group that hit The Colony.

I glanced to Nila, who passed the baby back to Ben, and with a look of sheer utter rage, loaded a magazine into her weapon.

I stopped the van to avoid running over the downed gate, and Nila jumped out.

"She'll be fine," Ben said.

I was sure she would be, but I still put the van in park and got out.

Nila, as if she were in a video game, aimed and fired, taking them all out alone. One shot to each deader as she walked across the property. She didn't head to the cabin. I knew where she was going.

I followed, and found one more deaders on the back porch; without missing a beat, Nila shot it and kept walking.

She headed straight to the cemetery created at the cabin.

She exhaled loudly, dropping her arm as she looked at the graves.

All the markers were still there.

The graves were untouched.

"At least they had the decency to leave my family alone." She holstered her weapon and walked by me.

It was a game of chasing Nila.

Ben and Finn were on the property when we walked around.

"Ben, why don't you and Finn get the generator? We'll try to get the property in some order," Nila said. "We'll remove the deaders and rig the fence. Then try to radio out."

"Nila," Finn said. "It's been raided. The radio is probably gone."

Nila shook her head. "I'm confident it's not."

"We've been raided before," Ben said. "No one's ever found our hiding place."

That was true. It was before my time with them, but true, however, these guys were pros, and I had my doubts. Especially after I stepped inside the cabin.

As I thought, they were pros. They didn't rampage through destroying everything. Granted things were a mess, but nothing was destroyed. It reminded me of when I was a cop, and we'd hear about drug busts and raids. Couch cushions removed, mattress overturned. They took pillows, blankets, pots and pans. Even the glass canning jars we left behind because they were too heavy to carry, they were now gone.

They removed everything they could to look beneath, except that damn throw rug that covered the hatch. Slightly crooked from being stepped on, a little folded at the ends, but still in place.

Everything we had stashed underneath in the floor storage was still there.

Including the radio.

Finn took that right away to try and reach out to those who survived The Colony attack, and if not them, the Nashville Colony.

I just wanted to get the kids inside and calm.

Nila and I definitely differed in what we saw at the cabin. I saw a cabin in disarray. Still, the fence was an easy fix, and the cabin was a safe place to be. Nila was livid and that probably was an understatement.

She went off for fifteen minutes about how someone defecated on the back porch with the outhouse six feet away. Her mood was horrible, and understandably so. She had a hell of a day. Searching for her baby, believing even for a short time that he had died, then coming to find her home had been raided.

It was hard to keep all the kids calm especially when they fed off of Nila's mood. She paced, drank whiskey straight from a bottle that was tucked in that hatch, and bitched. With every failed attempt Finn had to make radio contact, she grew more frustrated and hit that bottle harder, as if making up for lost drinking time.

Finally, the kids settled after we ate. The baby went down in a makeshift cradle we made out of a drawer.

And as we adults began to make plans for the next day, Finn returned announcing he'd made contact.

We were all ears listening to what he had to say.

"They're on their way to the Nashville Colony," Finn stated. "We lost about sixty people. Right now, my men are checking for the parents of four of the kids. If we can't locate them, they'll be placed in care down in Nashville."

Ben asked, "What about just sending them to Alaska. Are people still going?"

Finn nodded. "The convoy to Texas is still leaving as planned. We may have a few more people in there. We just need to head that way tomorrow."

"Is there any way to get me to Maryland?" Almada asked. "I need to get to those labs."

With a sharp turn and her arms folded across her chest, Nila gasped out a shocked, "What? You can't possibly still want to work with them when they tried to steal my child?"

"Nila," Almada spoke calmly. "I know you're upset, but I still need to find a cure. I need to end this so future generations never have to face this again. We fix it, we end it."

"I find it hard to believe that you can only do this with those assholes and Rosen in Maryland," Nila said.

Almada defended herself. "I am not doing this for or with Rosen. I am doing this for the future."

"And you can't do this somewhere else?" Nila asked. "Why would you not want to go to Alaska to work on this when you'll have the baby right there if you need anything?"

Finn bobbed his head up and down. "She has a point, Almada."

"You're not helping," I said, then saw Nila getting angrier and thought maybe if I interjected. "Nila, maybe the equipment she needs is only in Maryland."

Nila chuckled sarcastically. "Like Maryland is the holy grail of equipment."

Almada held up her hand. "It's not the holy grail of equipment, it's just that we found what we needed and built it there."

"Then find it elsewhere," Nila snapped. "And put it in fucking Alaska."

"Nila," Ben spoke with warning.

"No," she barked. "After everything they did, making her out to be the bad guy, she wants to work with them."

"I want to create the gene therapy cure. It's the only way," Almada said.

Nila shook her head. "I think it's time to give up the pipe dream. There will never be a workable cure. We'll never beat this. We'll all die out."

I stepped to Nila. "I know you're angry."

"Angry?" She huffed and shook her head. "Sean, did you hear Finn? They all just ran away and are headed to Nashville. They let these looting assholes just have The Colony."

"What should we have done?" Finn asked.

"Take them out," Nila snapped. "There are what? Two dozen? Fuck, give me a high-powered rifle with a scope, put me on a roof and I'll sniper their asses out myself."

"We will take them out," Finn said calmly. "We have a plan. Or, at least, they *said* there's a plan."

"When?" Nila asked. "When? When they've destroyed everything and moved on to the next colony? Are you gonna keep running?"

"Maybe," Almada said. "If I can get this virus under control, they won't have the dead to gather."

"Take them out," Nila said. "Take them out now, sooner than later before they hit again."

A usually mild-mannered Ben, suddenly spoke up with a sharp tone. "Then what, Nila? Then what?"

Nila turned to him. "Then move on and rebuild."

"Until the next group of bad guys comes along," Ben said. "And they take them out."

Ben shook his head. "Listen to what you're saying. Do you think it's that easy? You just want to create another poisoned well situation."

Nila gasped.

"That's exactly what you're trying to do," Ben argued. "Face it, Nila. Marauders came, they raided us, they hurt Lev, and you did what? Took them out. You poisoned the well. You killed all those people, Nila, and what happened? Here we are facing another group of bad people. We take them out, guaranteed another will take their place. Why? This...this is the world we live in now. There will be people who live and act like savages and take, kill, do whatever. In fact, wait...it was like that before the dead took over. There are good people and bad people, you have to decide which side of the line you are going to stand on. Which side do you want your children to see you on?"

"So, be weak and let them take everything?" Nila asked.

"No, be strong and find a way to survive."

"Ben, these people destroyed the cabin," Nila said. "They destroyed our home."

"Did they?" Ben asked. "I didn't know your father Nila, but from what I learned of Earl from you and Katie, I find it hard to believe that he would want you to sacrifice your humanity for this cabin. He built this cabin as his escape from the everyday life. You came to this cabin to escape the hell the world had become. Home is where you spend time with people you love, where you are with those most important. That's home. This cabin is not home."

"I understand what you're saying, Ben, I do," said Nila. "But we don't live in a world where we can be passive."

"True." Ben nodded. "We live in a time where we have a chance to not let this world dictate who we become. Do we let a savage world make us savage, or do we let a savage world make us better human beings? We talk about the future, well, we need to set a legacy for the future. That doesn't start years from now, that starts now. By moving on, being better people, keeping our humanity, and like your father did, building that sanctuary."

"Alaska," Nila said.

"Maybe. Maybe not. But we have to try." Ben stepped to her. "Nila, you have always been more than poisoning the well. Think about it. And…I'll take this." He reached out, took the bottle from her hand and walked away.

I saw it on Nila's face. She heard his words. We all did. Ben was passionate, and his words appealed to our humanity and resonated with us all.

Nila was going to go to Alaska, or try to get there, no matter what.

We would follow whatever she did.

Nila was our leader.

And right then and there, in the after-flurry of Ben's impassioned words, I believed was the moment Nila would choose which path she would lead us on to Alaska.

The vengeful angry one or the hopeful one.

THIRTY-SIX

A HOME TO LEAVE

Nila

March 2

I thought I was the first one awake the next morning; I opened my eyes just as the sun hit the horizon. My head pounded from drinking too much. I felt like an idiot for my anger, especially since, although it was in pain, my head was clear.

The cabin didn't look that bad, and I hated that I behaved so emotionally over it.

It wasn't the smartest thing to do, either. Drink a lot with an infant depending on me. Ben took my bottle, and took my baby.

Little Lev was in the drawer next to Ben; Ben was on the floor, cradling an empty baby bottle as if he fell asleep right after feeding time.

I smelt the coffee, it had a bitter scent and as I hit the kitchen, I saw Finn on the back porch. There was a medium saucepan on the stove with a ladle and when I passed it, I realized it was the coffee.

There were still mugs in the cabinets, I guess the looters didn't need them. I grabbed one out of the cabinet, and took a ladle of the brew.

It was bitter, but it was slightly hot coffee, and I needed it.

I took my mug outside and it was surprisingly warm.

"Is this a lone morning or can I join you?"

"You can join me. I'm just watching the sun, and the edge of the street."

"It feels warm," I said.

"It does.'

"Thanks for making coffee."

"I did the best I could." Finn brought his mug to his lips and sipped. "How are you feeling?"

"Like I learned a few lessons."

"You had a really emotional day yesterday," Finn said. "You didn't eat, and no one blames you or is angry with you for anything you said."

"Not even Almada?" I took another swig of my coffee.

"Not even her." He paused and looked out again. "I don't think we could have asked for a better day to travel. If we can find some gas, we'll be good."

"And the survivors are going to Nashville?" I asked.

"They are. I am hoping we can find some of the parents. If not, I'll make sure the kids are fine."

"You don't want to go to Alaska?"

Finn shook his head. "No, someone has to stay behind to keep you guys updated, make this place better again so you can come home."

"Finn, can I ask you something?"

"Sure."

"When this thing all started, we heard about Canada," I said. "We went and it was a disaster, and deadly, and eventually the virus and dead hit there. I didn't understand because they were stringent on who they let in."

"So, you're wondering if it's the same thing."

I nodded.

"Alaska is fine," he replied. "It's taken this long for them to be able to open their harbors and screen people effectively. You have a lot of areas out west that weren't hit as hard as us. At this point, I don't know if they ever will get it like we did. Still a lot of people out there, so who knows? The only way to ensure that eighty percent of a population won't wipe out again is to beat what threatened it in the first place."

"Unless another comes along."

"Once in every generation a plague will come," Finn stated.

"Is that the bible?" I asked, knowing he was a deacon.

"Nope. Stephen King."

I chuckled.

"Historically speaking, we can't stop another plague or virus," he said. "It's a pattern and always will be that way. Something big hits every eight to twelve years. I'd tell you to look it up but there's no more Google. So, you'll just have to trust me on it. And the more people there are the more it takes."

"This one was big."

"This was huge. But there's still a lot of people left." He faced me. "I can't promise you Alaska will be a bed of roses and I can't promise you another plague won't fall in our lifetime. I can promise you this though: I will do everything in my power, so that one day, in your lifetime, you can come back here to this cabin. Across a countryside that is safe again. I'll do my best."

I listened to him, and I believed him, not because he sounded sincere, but because I *wanted* to believe him.

After finishing our coffee, we woke everyone and hit the road. We secured the cabin again, as well as the fence. Securing it for the next bunch of looters that came through. I couldn't dwell on that though. I had to move forward.

While I had a night's sleep to think about the things Ben said, Almada thought about what I had said even in my angry, slightly intoxicated state.

She told me, "You're right. I can make the cure in Alaska. It's not like they're a third world country."

I hugged her when she told me and apologized as well. "Who knows," I said. "Maybe that's where the holy grail is?"

Too often on the journey since the virus hit, I led the way and chose the path. As we left the cabin, I made another decision. Until we arrived safely in Alaska, I was going to follow the path that led us instead of taking control.

That path led us to Nashville without incident, and to a good night's sleep, that was preceded by great food and music. In the morning a convoy of eight vehicles headed west to Texas and to the airport. We followed behind with Baby Lev in a brand-new infant seat provided by the colony.

Getting on that plane was scary. It was basic, quiet. One hundred and eighty-two people boarded.

The kids were excited, as if they were taking some sort of trip to dystopian Disney World. Perhaps in some way they were.

Sean was good with them all. He remained calm, while I was nervous and sipped on a tiny bottle of wine. More than I liked to admit, I picked up some habits from my stepmother, who drank Jack Daniels like it was a juice box.

June wanted to be a big girl, and she sat between Almada and Katie.

Unlike his father, James was the worldly traveler. He named places he had been with his aunt and uncle. He had a good life before us, and Lev would be happy about that.

Ben rested back, and his eyes closed before we took off. I didn't understand how he could be so calm, and I asked him.

"Nila, can you stop the plane from crashing or falling from the sky?"

"Great, thanks for that. Crashing wasn't why I was nervous," I replied. "But the answer to your question is no."

"We're here. We're going. No point getting anxiety."

He was right. Ben was right a lot.

I buckled my belt tight, sipped my wine and exhaled a lot.

"We have this," Sean said. "A new start. But we will come back."

I didn't see how that was possible. We were going north into the wild. We'd be trapped there somehow, at least that was what I thought.

But Sean and Finn believed it, so I held on to that.

Then I held onto Ben's hand as we took off.

THIRTY-SEVEN

A HOME FOR NOW

Nila

March 8

The first real sign of normal civilization hit us when we landed in Seattle. It still reminded me of a glorified colony. There were military-style fences all around the place, and newer buildings, erected in a huge open field that served as dorms until we would board the ship that would take us to Alaska.

We would be at the dorms for a couple days. Our flight, full of people from the colonies, was the only registered list of refuges, as we were called, going. They were ready for us with buses when we arrived. I was impressed.

I didn't see any dead, and we were far removed from the actual city of Seattle, so I couldn't see how much damage was done there.

They didn't say much to us other than there would be liaisons from Alaska on the ship to answer any questions, if we had any, and of course, more people would be there to help when we docked.

The Seattle dorms weren't bad, but they weren't great either, in fact they were rather boring for us. The ship was better. It was a cruise ship, and there were games for the kids, along with movies. Lots of old movies and television shows. Our liaison, Roger, told us that they were 'real big' on movies in Alaska and to get ready, entertainment was a plenty.

We all had little cabins on the same floor or whatever they call it on a ship. Me, Katie, James and the baby shared one. I always wanted to take a cruise, and this was quite different than my pre-deader world expectations. There were no plentiful buffets, pretty drinks, or eccentric entertainment.

The three-day cruise was preparation for what we would face in Alaska. I would be lying if I said I didn't worry that it would be a repeat of Canada, especially after they told us we would be in a quarantine center for ten days before being integrated and given a place to stay, jobs to do.

Except for Almada, they were all too aware of who she was and what she meant.

She would be given special treatment, a work area during her quarantine to start, and then she would head to Anchorage where she would immediately recreate the cure she made with Katie.

Finn assured her that they would get her the data she needed to continue her work, and of course she had my children to provide the samples she needed.

We registered Almada as part of our family fold when we arrived at Juneau, our quarantine port. Three adults and five children, we were the biggest family unit to venture together.

Our interview with Roger before docking reminded me of the first intake we had with The Colony.

Only no blood tests.

"Just medical treatment if needed," Roger said. "No need to test your blood unless you show signs of the virus."

I asked, "Has there been anyone that made it to Alaska that was sick."

Roger nodded. "Yes, and we handle it very humanely. Ben has told me what you and your daughter experienced in the early days of border crossing, so it's understandable that you might be worried about that. But it's different here. Those were the early days when people didn't know what to do, when they panicked and would do anything to try and stop the virus spread. I can't pretend to know what all of you went through. I have been extremely fortunate that I was in Alaska."

"No outbreaks at all?" Sean questioned.

Roger shook his head. "None. After about two weeks, all major news outside of Alaska went down. The military sent planes to check on things. We were cut off. It had to be horrific for you, losing so many, facing the monsters. By the time it reached the west coast, they were more prepared. They still suffered losses, and we know it took a long time to help. But taking people in right away without the right preparations and before everyone was ready would have bred the same disaster Eastern Canada experienced when they tried to help people."

I understood what Roger was saying, and when we finally docked in Juneau, I could see he wasn't misleading us.

Volunteers with blue vests and paper facemasks greeted us warmly with boxes and gifts.

The quarantine center was more of a camp with FEMA style trailers and mobile homes.

Roger would spend time in quarantine as well, just in case he was exposed. He would be there to help us and get us ready to move on.

He seemed compassionate, honest enough, and interested in our stories. The same stories he'd probably heard a hundred times. He showed the most excitement when he found out Ben was a doctor as well, and Sean a former policeman. It would be easy to get them into jobs. If I didn't want to work, I didn't need to because I had small children.

I let him know that I wanted to work, and that I would be a productive member of society. When he asked what I did before and when I told him Arby's, he smiled brightly.

"Oh, customer service, you must be a people person."

To which Ben, Sean and Almada all responded with a "No."

I always thought I was, but the world took that from me.

Everything had changed so much, so fast and so many times.

Here we were again, about to make another change.

The state of Alaska had been through their own changes as well. They were self-reliant in all aspects: food, fuel, and energy. Not that they weren't before, but they couldn't rely on imports now. Things were moving forward except, Roger said, with entertainment.

But that would come. Until then there were plenty of old movies and television shows.

I was glad, because I wanted Katie, Sawyer, June, James, and Lev to know what the world was like before, even if it was watching reruns. To see what they had to work to rebuild and bring back.

Even though I knew I would miss the cabin, I felt surprisingly good about the move to Alaska.

It was odd, arriving to a bright, shiny, untouched land.

Like waking up from a nightmare or driving through a horrendous storm and suddenly it was light.

I couldn't be angry that they never sent troops in to help us or feed us, I could only be grateful that they kept things alive. Had they done it soon, like Roger said, it would have been bad. Then there wouldn't have been a bright spot, an end of the tunnel light such as we faced at the end of our journey.

But it wasn't the end.

It was a beginning. I wondered if that part of me, the people person, the woman who loved binge watching shows, would she return?

I doubted that. I'd lost so much, so many people I loved and adored. Despite how hard I would try, I would forever be tainted by the loss and pain, along with the horrific things I had seen.

There was hope for the children though, I knew that. Especially if Almada really did accomplish a cure.

Memories would fade for Katie and Sawyer, maybe even James. June and Lev would never remember any of it and that was a good thing.

Like the civil war was for me, the Deader Virus and the devastation would be pages on a history book to them.

We can't erase what happened, we can only learn from it.

I would love to say that I hoped that my children could make the world a better place this time, but after all we had been through and where we ended up, I didn't think we'd have to wait that long. It was already getting better.

THIRTY-EIGHT

BACK HOME

Katie

Fifteen years later

"Yes, Katie, yes, we hear you fine." My mother glanced over her shoulder to me from the front seat.

Then Sean, who was driving, did his typically passive thing with her. "Nila, come on she's just excited."

"She's a grown ass woman," my mother barked.

That made me laugh. I laughed a lot.

Of course I was, it was the moment I had been waiting forever for.

I was excited, and I did feel like a kid again, filled with excitement and thrilled, the same way I felt every time we'd go to Anchorage to visit Almie.

It had been fifteen years since we arrived in Alaska, and eight years since the cure was widely available.

The virus still rears its ugly head, and there had been several outbreaks in Alaska, but nothing devastating and always brought under control.

Was it over?

That remained to be seen, there was always a chance it could happen again.

But we'd be ready.

More than the years that had passed since making Alaska our home, it had been almost four years since the borders and ports were open, and the now Federation of America was safe. Advertisements were everywhere looking for new settlers, because, according to Finn, it was a pretty empty country.

It took three years to convince my mother to go. I didn't want to go without her. Once she finally relented, it took a year of planning.

Thank God for Finn's help.

Then again, he was the president of the FOA, and had been for ten years. I guess elections were a thing of the past. They'd say he was elected, but I knew that wasn't really the case. A military guy in charge made sense to a lot of people, and so there he was.

At one point James had made a joke, a rarity for him, exclaiming, "Oh my God, just make him king!"

I loved James. I loved everyone. I had become the eternally optimistic person that just was annoying as hell, and I knew it, but I didn't care.

I did it for Fleck. I thought of him every day of my life, he was embedded in my heart and soul and even though he was gone, wherever he was, I still wanted to annoy him.

Being optimistic would do that.

I tried not to annoy my mother though; she was a pretty tough one to crack.

I'm not sure why she changed so much in Alaska. The brave woman who shot first asked questioned later, and infamously poisoned the well, became mild mannered and settled.

But kind of cold. She really didn't smile too much or even cry.

I don't think she picked up a gun again, even during hunting season when they offered incentives.

My mother worked at the volunteer center to prove she was a people person.

She was. At the volunteer center.

At home, she played grandmother to Sawyer's son, cooked horrible meals, and binge watched old shows she had seen a hundred times.

Watching *The Walking Dead* was a comedic highlight in her life.

That was funny to me.

But she needed to go.

Even for the trip.

Finn and Sean both promised her that, one day, she could go back home.

Back to the cabin.

It was Sean that actually was the convincing factor, bringing up that promise he made her.

They were this weird couple. They got married on my tenth birthday, but I swore I never saw them show affection. Not even when the minister said, 'You may kiss,' they shook hands and gave this like, strained, barely touching hug.

Who knows?

They worked.

And because of Sean she was doing it. She said, "Okay, fine, Katie, I'll go."

Each mile we traveled I could see it on her face that she was happy and excited, despite what she said.

"Katie, it won't be there. Everything will be destroyed," she said.

"Fifteen years, Ma," I told her. "A lot of clean up and renewal."

Finn gave me progress reports and showed me pictures of America, so that was how I knew for certain it was going to be a good road trip.

We saw Finn a lot, usually twice a year he came to Alaska to check on things.

He would tell me stories and I couldn't wait for this day.

Now, I had it. A family road trip like they did in *Family Guy*. Only Sean wasn't anywhere near Peter Griffin, he was more like Cleveland.

I wanted Ben to come along, but he claimed his hip couldn't take the long journey. I think it was his wife that wouldn't let him go. He got remarried to this really young woman he met when he did surgery on her sister. He went back to plastic surgery, I guess even in a dystopian world people need boob jobs.

Sawyer didn't come either, which saddened me. He was funny. When we were younger, we'd watch *Family Guy* over and over, and laugh so hard we cried.

James was more of a *Law and Order* person. Of course, James was so serious. My mother couldn't believe how much he could be like the father he never met.

Convincing James to come along was almost as hard as convincing my mother. Only his excuse was work. He was a fisherman.

June and Lev were still in school, so we had to wait until summer break.

Neither knew about the world before the deaders.

215

They knew only Alaska and what they saw on the television shows. Lev was addicted to the show *Supernatural*, so much it took until he was thirteen for us to convince him there were no werewolves and vampires.

His argument was valid. He said if there were dead that walked, there could be werewolves.

June was weird. She was into cooking shows that streamed.

To her, life was a *MasterChef* kitchen and what she could create with fish.

Actually, she was really a great cook.

Someone had to be, my mother never was.

At least June knew what to do with her life and she was only seventeen.

Me, I still didn't know. I didn't go to college and bounced from job to job. My mother suggested something artistic. I gave up drawing when I learned to decipher the messages I was seeing in my head.

Nothing held my interest for long. Eventually something would, I just hadn't found it yet.

I wished there was still an Arby's, that sounded cool.

But I did have something. The trip.

That had my interest.

We as family were all together, going somewhere special.

We took a ship to Vancouver and from there it was a two-day train to Toronto where Finn was waiting because he was there on some sort of leader business.

He had a van for us, and we loaded in.

It wouldn't be long before we'd be back.

We would meet up with him. I swore he was as excited as me about our family vacation. When I asked him why, he only responded that he was happy that my mom could see he kept his promise.

We loaded in the van, Mom and Sean in the front. James and Lev in the middle seat and I was in the back with June.

I wanted to take in as much of the view as I could. It was so different. We weren't on a road trip running for our lives. The deaders weren't roaming here and there, cars were no longer scattered on the highway.

No burnt buildings, no destroyed cities.

It was green.

Lush and big trees lined the roads, they were so beautiful it was breathtaking.

Nothing, absolutely nothing was the same.

To me it looked like a different country, or we had taken a trip back in time to when it was all new. Before man, living and dead, destroyed it.

A lot of the highways were cleared and redone. But there was no traffic.

"Right up here," I said, looking at the map. "That's the road. Can you hear me?"

"Yes," my mother replied. "We aren't a hundred feet away from you."

James sighed out. "You should have sat here."

"I can see way better back here." I glanced down to the map. "Are you turning, Sean?"

"Right now," Sean replied.

I heard the click, click.

"Oh my God, he used a turn signal. That's so funny. In *Family Guy*—"

"Please," James cut me off. "Please stop talking about *Family Guy*. I realize that was the only show you watched for a decade, but please, no more."

"It's funny."

"No, it's not."

"How would you know?" I flung out my hand. "You don't laugh."

"Guys," Sean warned.

"You like *Family Guy*, right?" I asked June. "Especially the one episode where Peter was a chef."

"Oh, yeah, that was good," June replied. "All the butter."

"See." I nudged James. "And one day Lev will like it too."

"Nah, I doubt it," my brother Lev said. "I'm more of a *Simpsons* guy."

I was about to comment when I heard my mother say something about it being odd.

"What is?" I asked.

"The road," she answered. "The private road to the cabin, it should have been long overgrown. It's not."

Sean made the turn.

I remembered the road well, even though I was young.

How many times we went up and down it.

The van bounced a few times with the bumps in the road, but it was still a road of sorts.

Then Sean stopped.

When he did, my mother released an intense sob and opened the door, almost falling out of the van.

What was it? Had the cabin fallen down? Been destroyed?

We all hurried from the van, and I saw my mother standing in front of a perfect fence.

I expected the cabin to be hidden with fifteen years' worth of weeds and trees. But it wasn't.

It looked like the day we left, only better, more like when we lived there.

James, Lev, June and I followed my mother as she opened the gate.

That was when I saw the note.

"Welcome back." The note read. It was from Finn.

He not only kept his promise that my mother could come home, he made sure she had a cabin to come home to.

It was a surprise for me as well, the property was in pristine condition.

My mother could barely walk she was overcome with emotions. She turned and fell into Sean's arms, and he held her for a second before he said, "Let's go see them."

And they walked off.

James shifted his eyes to me. "Did they just…hug?"

"Yeah, weird, I know." I motioned for my brothers and sister to follow me.

I knew where my mother and Sean were going. Behind the cabin to the little cemetery. They were still holding each other when we arrived.

So strange for them.

But I saw why.

The graves had been maintained, and there were two additional markers next to them. My brother Earl and Fleck.

When I saw it, I wanted to cry out a huge thank you to Finn. I wasn't sure why he did all that he did, maybe he found a purpose in the cabin, visiting it often to maintain, or maybe he did it right before we arrived, when I told him about the trip.

It didn't matter.

I was expecting nothing and was given a gift. A gift of a memory I thought would be erased by time and nature and I got to see my mother genuinely happy.

We would be at the cabin for a week, but somehow, I suspected my mother wouldn't want to leave.

I know I didn't.

I loved Alaska and my life there, but I was finally home.

Really home.

I felt it, I knew it.

We had come full circle.

I watched everything around me crumble and die and now it was living and thriving.

Mother Nature cleaned up our mess and presented us with a clean slate.

I knew at that moment, staring at the graves, looking back at not only the cabin, but my grandfather's pride and joy, that we really did it.

We made it through.

No longer was it a dead world, it was our world.

We finally took it back.

<><> THE END <><>

Jacqueline Druga is a native of Pittsburgh, PA. Her works include genres of all types but she favors post-apocalypse and apocalypse writing.

For updates on new releases you can find the author on:
Facebook: @jacquelinedruga
Twitter: @gojake
www.jacquelinedruga.com